The Home School Detectives

THE MYSTERY OF THE
MISSING MICROCHIPS

John Bibee

INTERVARSITY PRESS
DOWNERS GROVE, ILLINOIS 60515

InterVarsity Press® is the book-publishing division of InterVarsity Christian Fellowship®, a student movement active on campus at hundreds of universities, colleges and schools of nursing in the United States of America, and a member movement of the International Fellowship of Evangelical Students. For information about local and regional activities, write Public Relations Dept., InterVarsity Christian Fellowship, 6400 Schroeder Rd., P.O. Box 7895, Madison, WI 53707-7895.

Cover illustration: David Darrow

ISBN 0-8308-1912-6

Printed in the United States of America ♾

Library of Congress Cataloging-in-Publication Data has been requested.

15	14	13	12	11	10	9	8	7	6	5	4	3	2
06	05	04	03	02	01	00	99	98	97	96			

Chapter One

Trapped!

Don't drop me!" Billy Renner cried, his voice echoing inside the big metal dumpster.

"I won't drop you," Carlos yelled back. He gripped Billy's legs more tightly. "At least I don't think I will. Quit wiggling your legs so much."

"I can't help it. Slide me in a little further. I want to turn over a box. I think I can get it then."

Carlos and Billy were looking in the dumpster behind the Springdale Toystore. The children had been down at the *Springdale Gazette,* the local newspaper, doing research for a home school project on the town's history around the turn of the century. The object was to report on what everyday life was like in each decade in Springdale. They were studying the years from 1900 to 1910 first.

Mrs. Highsmith, the chief reporter at the *Gazette,* was a friend and a big help. She had gotten to know the children earlier that year when they helped solve a thirty-year-old robbery in Springdale involving stolen money and treasure. She had written about them in the newspaper, dubbing them the Home School Detectives. No one could have guessed that a new mystery was going to start that day.

The children had worked in the basement of the *Gazette* for almost two hours. They had planned to meet at the Dairy Queen afterward for ice cream cones. Billy, Rebecca and Carlos had stopped at the toystore to see if a new computer game had arrived. Then they planned to take home a few empty boxes for Carlos, who wanted to use them to store his rapidly expanding chemistry set.

Rebecca was still in the toystore when Billy and Carlos went to the alley to look for boxes. Carlos had already found two good boxes, but then Billy had started exploring in the dumpster on his own. He had uncovered the edge of what looked like a hamster cage. He was determined to discover if the cage was any good or not. Carlos had agreed to help.

"I still can't reach it. Slide me in some more," Billy hollered over his shoulder.

"Hurry up," Carlos said. "I can almost taste the chocolate-dipped cone I'm going to get."

Carlos tipped Billy farther over the edge into the dumpster. The two wooden crates he was standing on wobbled. He shifted his feet and braced himself when a bee appeared out of nowhere. Carlos jerked back his head as the large yellow and black bumblebee dived down at his black hair.

"Get away!" Carlos yelled, twisting his head, trying to locate the bee. The buzzing got louder and softer several times as the bee circled the boy's head. Then the buzzing stopped. Carlos was relieved. He gripped Billy's legs tighter. Then he felt something prickly moving on top of his head. He froze. The little feet on his head seemed very busy surveying the top of "Mount Carlos."

"Slide me in just a little more!" Billy yelled out. "I almost got it."

"Aaacccckkkk!" Carlos screamed. With an automatic reflex, he swatted at his hair frantically. As the bee buzzed away, he realized he had let go of Billy's legs. Out of the corner of his eye he saw Billy's feet disappear over the edge of the dumpster. As Billy fell, his foot hit the lid which clanged down shut on top of him.

The big bee suddenly returned and dive-bombed Carlos. He danced around the alley, swatting wildly. He was still jerking and jumping when Rebecca Renner, Billy's sister, rode up on her bicycle. She stopped and watched Carlos curiously.

"Are you okay?" she asked as Carlos finally settled down.

"Is it gone? Do you see it? Is it gone?" He leaned over so Rebecca could see the top of his head.

"See what?"

"The bee. A giant bumblebee. I bet it was big as a tennis ball. Is it gone?"

"I don't see anything." Rebecca looked at his head. "Where's Billy?"

"Get me out of here!" a muffled voice yelled from within the dumpster, followed by a pounding noise on the metal side.

"Is Billy in there?" Rebecca asked.

"Oooops," Carlos said, looking at the dumpster.

"It's dark!" the voice yelled. "Get me out of here!"

Carlos jumped up on the crates and lifted the lid. For a moment, it seemed stuck. Then it opened. Billy's head popped up in front of Carlos. The younger boy squinted at the sunlight and then glared at Carlos. Billy rubbed his ears, trying to make the ringing sound go away.

"Sorry," Carlos said meekly.

"You dropped me," Billy accused his friend.

"I couldn't help it. A gigantic bumblebee landed right on top of my head."

"What bumblebee?" Billy asked doubtfully.

"A bee! A bee!" Rebecca screamed out. She jumped off her bike and hopped around in the alley, flailing her arms in the air. She ran toward Carlos. As she did, Carlos and Billy saw the bee racing after her.

"Duck!" Billy yelled. Carlos leaned back. The crates he was standing on wobbled. Carlos jerked back further and suddenly he was falling backward and sideways into Billy's arms. Both boys tumbled down inside the big dumpster.

"Don't leave me alone!" Rebecca yelled out when she saw Carlos and Billy disappear. The buzzing bee sounded louder than a chain saw. She ran for the dumpster. She used the crates as a step, grabbed the metal edge, pulled herself up and flipped into the dumpster, trying to escape the angry insect.

"Look out!" she yelled as she flew through the air. Billy and Carlos barely had time to scoot out of the way. Rebecca hit a cardboard box, which collapsed under her weight as it broke her fall. Before anyone could speak, the big metal lid fell down with a deafening clang. The noise died away. For a moment, everything was quiet inside the dark dumpster.

"Good night, it's dark in here," Rebecca said as she struggled to sit up.

"You're on my leg!" Carlos yelled.

"I can't see anything," Rebecca replied.

"I can't see either," Billy said. "Why did you close the lid?"

"I didn't close the lid. It fell," Rebecca replied crossly. "I bet I've got hearing loss from the noise."

"How do you think I feel?" Billy asked. "It happened to me twice. You guys are crazy. First, Carlos jumps on me and then my own sister."

"I didn't jump. I fell," Carlos said, trying to sit up. "That big bee was coming right at me."

"What bee?"

"A bumblebee as big as a bird," Rebecca said. "It came after me too. I thought it was going to crawl right inside my ear. I thought Carlos was trying to hide in here. I didn't want to be the only one left out there fighting that monster. Didn't you see it?"

"The only thing I saw was Carlos and then your big feet. Let's get out of this thing."

"Right." Carlos struggled to stand up in the darkness. "There's a crack of light where the lid is warped."

"Open it up," Billy said. "I feel like a sardine in here."

"At least it's not very smelly," Rebecca said. "Toystore garbage is clean garbage."

Carlos pushed against the heavy metal lid. It rose a few inches and then stopped.

"Open it up," Billy repeated.

"I'm trying," Carlos grunted.

"What do you mean, you're trying?" Rebecca demanded.

"I mean I'm pushing as hard as I can, and it won't open," Carlos said.

"What?" Rebecca asked in alarm.

"Of course it will open."

"Then why isn't it?" Rebecca demanded.

"Because it's . . . stuck or something." Carlos quit pushing. His arms ached.

"Stuck?" Billy asked. "You mean we're stuck in here?"

"Quit kidding around, Carlos," Rebecca said.

"I'm not kidding," Carlos replied in his calm, even tone. Carlos, who wanted to be a scientist when he grew up, had a sense of humor, but Rebecca and everyone else knew he wasn't a practical joker.

"You mean we're really stuck?" Billy asked. "That's kind of cool."

"Billy!" Rebecca moaned. "It is not cool. This could be dangerous."

"At least we don't have to worry about that bee," Carlos said.

"It's just a little dark," Billy said. "The crack is big enough for us to breathe. We aren't going to suffocate or anything."

"But how are we going to get out?" Rebecca asked.

"Let's see," Carlos said. "Is there a latch or something that holds the lid down?"

"I don't remember any latch." Billy stood up slowly until the top of his head was pressing against the lid. He pushed up the lid with his hands and head. The lid rose two inches and then stopped. The extra light inside the dumpster made them all feel much better.

"See if there are any dangling metal bars or anything like that along the sides," Carlos said.

"I see a limousine down the alley," Billy said. "Look over there, four dumpsters down."

All the children looked. A long black limousine rolled to a stop between two dumpsters about twenty-five yards away. As they watched, a man with short blond hair wearing a dark suit got out of the driver's side and went around to the rear of the car. He opened the trunk.

"If we yell, maybe he could hear us," Rebecca said.

"No, wait," Carlos whispered. "Look at him."

The man paused, looking nervously up and down the alley. He then bent down into the trunk and lifted up a cardboard box with a red and blue stripe on the side. He carried the box over to a dumpster and dropped it in. He went back to the trunk of the car. He carried another identical box over to the same garbage container and dumped it. He ran back to the car and closed the trunk. He leaned against the back of the car, as if waiting.

"What's he doing?" Becky asked.

"Ssshhh," Carlos said. They heard the sound of a car coming down the alley. An old red pickup truck drove slowly past the dumpster that held the three children. The back of the pickup truck was covered with a blue tarp. The man by the limousine stood up straight as he watched the pickup approach. He stuck his right hand into a pocket of his suit jacket and looked around the alley nervously.

A man dressed in blue jeans and an old blue shirt got out of the pickup. He wore a cowboy hat and had a big mustache.

"Look!" Billy whispered. "Mr. Cowboy Hat has a big brown envelope. I bet it's full of drug money."

As Carlos tried to hush Billy, the man in the suit took the envelope from Mr. Cowboy Hat. The two men talked. The man in the suit looked in the envelope and then tossed it into the limousine. He then opened the trunk of the car and lifted out another cardboard box with a red and blue stripe on the side. Mr. Cowboy Hat took the box. He looked inside it for a few moments. He closed the flaps on the box. Then, the two men began to argue. Mr. Dark Suit kept shaking his head as Mr. Cowboy Hat wagged a finger at him.

"What's Mr. Dark Suit up to? Trying to pull a double-cross, I'd say," Billy whispered.

"I don't know," Carlos said. All he could hear was the tone of the words, not the actual words themselves.

Suddenly, the man in the suit ran and got back inside the limousine. Mr. Cowboy Hat started after the man and dropped the box. The limousine took off. Mr. Cowboy Hat hurriedly picked up the box, not seeming to notice that something had spilled out. He ran to his truck and got inside. The pickup truck screeched down the alley after the limousine. Both vehicles turned left when they reached the street.

"I wonder why they left so fast?" Rebecca said.

A third car, a dark blue sedan, then cruised quickly down the alley. Three men were inside of it. It never stopped until it reached the end of the alley. It also turned left, its tires screeching.

"What's going on?" Rebecca asked the others.

"I just know it was something illegal," Billy said.

"You may be right," Carlos said solemnly.

"The Home School Detectives are on another case!" Billy said gleefully. "Wait till we tell Josh, Emily and Julie about this. We need to get those boxes from that other dumpster first. I wonder if it's money or drugs that's inside them!"

"Aren't you forgetting something?" Rebecca asked.

"What?"

"We're stuck in here. We aren't going anywhere."

"Josh and the others will be looking for us if we don't show up at the Dairy Queen," Billy said confidently. "At least I think they'll look for us. After all, we have music practice tonight."

"That's hours from now," Rebecca moaned.

Down the alley, the children heard the sound of a large engine and squeaking brakes.

"Someone else is coming," Carlos said.

"Finally," Rebecca said with relief. "Let's yell as they drive by."

"Sounds like a big truck," Billy said.

"It's a garbage truck," Carlos said, peering out through the crack in the lid.

"Garbage truck?" Rebecca asked. "Then he'll let us out."

"Uh oh," Carlos said, staring down the alley. The garbage truck stopped at the dumpster behind the shoestore. Two big metal arms lowered as the truck approached the dumpster. The arms slid into long square slots on two sides of the dumpster. Then the arms slowly lifted the big metal container up into the air over the front of the truck toward the back. As it continued tipping, the lid of the dumpster opened and all the trash and contents fell into the garbage trunk. The big arms then lowered the empty dumpster back down to the alley floor with a loud, metallic boom. The truck backed away and headed down the alley. The dumpster behind the toystore was next.

"Help!" Rebecca screamed, but the roar of the truck was too loud.

"Wait!" Carlos desperately tried to push up the lid on the garbage container. Billy was looking around in the dumpster for something he could stick through the edge to wave as a flag. The engine roared as the truck headed for the dumpster holding the three children. The big arms of the truck lowered as it approached.

"Help!" Rebecca screamed. The truck moved forward, the big arms aimed right for the garbage container. All the children screamed, but the roar of the approaching truck drowned out their cries.

Chapter Two

Missing!

I don't like the sound of those sirens," Julie Brown said, looking at her half-eaten ice cream cone. The police sirens had been wailing for several minutes. "I wonder what's keeping Carlos and the others? They said they would meet us here right after they stopped at the toystore."

"Maybe they went home," Emily Morgan replied, licking her chocolate-dipped cone. She took her time and savored each bite. She bit off the tip of the cone and then nibbled the edges of the chocolate in a circular pattern, around and around until she reached the crusty cone.

"Carlos and Billy wouldn't pass up a Dairy Queen," Julie Brown said. Carlos was her adopted brother.

"That's what I think," Josh said, noticing that Julie was really worried. "I guess we could go look for them."

"Where would you start?" Emily asked.

"I'd take the shortest route to the toystore from here, and

then go between there and the *Gazette* office," Josh said. "If we don't see them, we could call home and ask if they're there."

"They should be all right, don't you think?"

"It makes you wonder," Julie said. "I know Carlos wouldn't dilly-dally around too much when an ice cream cone was waiting. I guess hearing all those sirens makes me nervous."

"It's probably a fire or something," Josh said, trying to calm his friend. Julie was the most sensitive person he knew. She was also known for her hunches and intuition, which often turned out to be quite accurate.

Julie took off her glasses and cleaned them slowly with a napkin. She looked off in the distance. She ignored her ice cream cone, which had begun to drip down the sides onto the table.

"Let's go to the toystore," Julie said with a frown. "I still have a very weird feeling about this whole thing."

Her two friends nodded and quickly finished their cones. After they strapped on their backpacks and bike helmets, they began to pedal for the toystore.

As they got closer to the old downtown area of Springdale, Julie, who was in the lead, slowed down. Near the intersection ahead, two police cars were stopped in the road, their red and blue lights flashing around and around. Several orange fire flares sizzled on the pavement, blocking off the lane of traffic. A long black limousine was smashed up against a telephone pole.

"There's been some sort of accident," Julie said to the others. They pulled to the side of the road and stopped. "That's the reason we heard those sirens. I don't see any bicycles, do you?"

The children all craned their necks. A policeman was waving cars around the accident.

"It just looks like a big black limousine to me," Josh said. "I don't see any other cars. Look at those skid marks. They must go fifty feet. Whoever was driving was really moving fast."

"I hate accidents," Emily said. "I don't want to look, if anyone's hurt."

"I don't see anyone," Josh said. "Let's get closer."

The children rode their bicycles single file down the street, following the flow of traffic. The police officer waved them by.

"Hi, Julie," the officer said. It was Deputy Andy Haskins. He was a member of the Springdale Community Church, the same church all the other children attended, where Julie's father was pastor.

"Anyone hurt?" Julie asked, pedaling more slowly.

"We're not sure," Deputy Haskins said. "We can't find the driver of the car. There's a bullet hole in the side door, though."

"A bullet hole!" Julie said. She looked behind them. Since no cars were coming, she stopped. The others also stopped.

"You mean someone was shooting?" Josh asked. "Was there any . . . any blood or anything?"

"We found some blood on the door handle, but it wasn't very much," Deputy Haskins said slowly. "Sheriff Weaver's not sure what's going on. When we arrived, all we found was an empty car. No driver. We're trying to find witnesses and see if anyone knows anything."

"You haven't seen my brother, Carlos, or Billy or Rebecca Renner, have you?" Julie asked with concern.

"Can't say that I have," the deputy replied. "But we've been pretty busy since this call came in. By the way, you kids in the Servant's class at church sure did a good job picking up all that litter along Highway 17 last weekend. I heard lots of nice compliments down at the office."

"We had lots of help," Julie said.

"If I'm off duty the next time you go on a project, I want to be out there helping too."

"There's always room for more help," Josh said. "It's a lot of fun, really, especially when everyone works together."

"Well, you all better move along, a car is coming," the deputy said.

Julie started pedaling again, followed by Josh, then Emily. As they got closer to the old downtown section of Springdale, they turned onto Grand Street. They parked their bicycles carefully in front of the toystore. Julie Brown was the first one inside.

Mr. and Mrs. Grant, the owners of the Springdale Toystore, stood behind the counter. The Springdale Toystore had been in Mr. Grant's family for three generations. They were members of the Springdale Community Church too.

"Here are the famous Home School Detectives now!" Mrs. Grant said with a smile. "Where's the rest of the gang?"

"That's what we'd like to know," Julie said. "Did my brother and Billy and Rebecca Renner come in here earlier?"

"They sure did," Mr. Grant said. "Rebecca bought a new computer game and some batteries. The boys were just looking around. They went out back to the alley looking for boxes, and I'm guessing that she followed them."

"How long ago was that?" Josh asked.

"Must have been about an hour ago," Mrs. Grant said.

"They were supposed to meet us at the Dairy Queen and didn't show up," Julie said. "I'm sort of worried."

"You don't think they went somewhere else?" Mr. Grant asked kindly.

"That's what I think happened," Emily said. "You know Billy. He probably talked them into going over to the video arcade or someplace like that. I bet they're at the Dairy Queen right now wondering where we are."

"It could be," Mr. Grant said. "I'll tell you what. I'll give Jimmy a call."

"Thanks, Mr. Grant," Julie said. Mr. Grant dialed the number. He asked Jimmy, the owner of the Dairy Queen, about the missing children. Then he hung up.

"They haven't been there yet," Mr. Grant said. He looked kindly at Julie. "I wouldn't worry about them too much. They'll probably show up pretty soon."

"I hope so," Julie said. "This is more of a mystery than I like. I'm really beginning to get worried. I just have a feeling things aren't right, for some reason."

"This must be a day for mysteries," Mr. Grant said. "The police found a wrecked, abandoned car over on Thorndyke Avenue. A big black limousine."

"We rode past it," Josh said. "Deputy Haskins said they didn't find anyone there."

"But they found a bullet hole in the side of the car," Mrs. Grant said. "Isn't that something? Someone shooting right here in Springdale!"

"Were you listening on your police scanner?" Emily asked, perking up. She liked everything electronic. The more gadgets the better, as far as she was concerned.

"You can hear a lot on those scanners," Mr. Grant said with

a smile. "Those are amazing little gizmos. As soon as that call came in, I almost hopped into my Chrysler to go take a look myself. But you can learn plenty just sitting here listening as they talk about it."

"I wish I had a scanner," Emily said wistfully. "I've been saving my money."

"On the scanner, Sheriff Weaver said the driver may have been robbed and kidnapped," Mrs. Grant added dramatically. "A witness thinks he saw a blue sedan stop by the limousine and then move on."

"I wonder what happened?" Emily asked.

"We better keep moving," Josh said, looking at Julie's worried face. "Let's check out the alley."

"You kids be careful," Mr. Grant said. Julie was the first one out the door. They rode their bicycles back around to the alley.

"Hey, I see Carlos's bicycle!" Julie sped up. Carlos's bike was leaning against the rear wall of the toystore. "His backpack is on the seat."

"Billy and Rebecca's bikes are over there!" Josh pointed across the alley. "They left their backpacks too."

"Where are they then?" Emily asked. "They must be nearby if they left their bicycles and their backpacks."

"Carlos! Billy! Rebecca!" Josh's voice bounced up the old brick walls in the alley. He waited. No answer.

"That's odd," Julie said. "Why would they leave their bikes and backpacks in the alley?"

"They were going to look for some empty boxes." Josh walked over to the dumpster behind the toystore. He lifted up the metal lid and looked inside. "It's empty."

Julie ran over to the next dumpster. She stood on her tiptoes and looked inside. "This one is empty too."

"If all the trash has been picked up, maybe they went looking for boxes somewhere else," Josh said.

"But why would they leave their bikes and backpacks here?" Julie asked.

"That does seem sort of strange," Josh replied.

Emily walked down the alley. She looked in three other dumpsters. They were all empty. As she turned around to come back, she saw something in the middle of the alley. She bent down for a closer look. She picked up four dark objects and looked at them closely. She put three of them in her pocket and carried one in her hand.

"Hey, look what I found," Emily yelled out. She walked quickly toward the others.

Josh was looking inside Rebecca's backpack. "She even left the computer game in her backpack."

"I found something in the alley," Emily said excitedly.

"She left the computer game in her pack?" Julie asked, going over to Josh. "That's not like her. That game cost a lot of money."

"I found something, you guys," Emily repeated. Before the others could answer, a car turned into the alley. All the children moved to one side. A man wearing sunglasses drove the blue car slowly past the children. Another man sat in the passenger seat. He had a short red beard. The car moved down the alley. Then it stopped near two dumpsters behind the shoe store.

"What's he doing?" Josh whispered to the others.

The passenger got out of the car. He walked over to the dumpsters. He looked into one and then looked into the other. He rubbed his beard slowly, as if thinking. Then he looked in the first dumpster again. He stepped back and looked up and down the alley. He walked toward the children but stopped at the dumpster behind the pharmacy. He looked inside it. He slammed down the lid angrily. He checked the next dumpster and the next, walking up the alley, closer and closer to the children.

"He doesn't look very happy," Julie whispered.

"He's looking for something," Josh replied. "But what?"

"He's looking at us!" Emily whispered. The other children nodded. The man was looking right at them. He stared for a few moments and then slowly turned back toward his car. He got back in the passenger seat. The sedan moved down the alley. At the corner the car turned left and disappeared.

"I wonder what he was looking for?" Julie asked.

"I don't know," Josh replied. "He seemed upset that he didn't find it."

"I found something, you guys," Emily said. But Josh and Julie weren't listening. Josh was looking inside Billy's backpack and Julie was looking inside Rebecca's. Emily watched them.

Josh patiently took everything out of the backpack and laid it on the pavement. "I don't see a note or anything that would indicate where they've gone. Did you find anything?"

"Nothing yet." Julie spread the contents of Rebecca's backpack on a wooden crate.

"I found something up the alley where that guy was looking," Emily repeated. "Look, you guys!"

She held out her hand. A shadow covered it. She whirled around. The man with the red beard was staring down at her open hand. Josh and Julie jumped up when they saw him.

"I'd like to look at that," the man said. He reached for Emily's hand. He didn't smile.

Chapter Three

Taken for a Ride

When the garbage truck slammed into the side of the dumpster containing the three children, Billy covered his head with his hands. The long metal arms of the truck slid into the slots on the sides of the big metal container. The container slid across the alley pavement a few feet. The scraping metal and noise of the truck engine covered the cries of the three children inside the dumpster.

"Lord Jesus, help us!" Rebecca screamed as the dumpster was lifted off the pavement. The hydraulic arms whined as the driver of the truck revved the engine. The dumpster rose into the air, up over the hood of the truck.

"Try to hold on!" Carlos yelled to Billy and Rebecca. But the other children were busy enough just trying to keep some sort of balance as the big container swung through the air. Billy crouched in one corner of the dumpster, both hands braced against the metal walls. As the dumpster passed over the cab of the truck, it began to tip forward.

"Help!" Rebecca screamed again as the tiny world inside the trash container turned upside down. The children tumbled and lost all balance in the mounds of trash and boxes. It all happened so fast. The lid became the floor, and it popped open with a clang. Trash, boxes and three children fell out of the dumpster into the rear of the garbage truck.

"Look out!" Billy yelled. But the fall wasn't as far as he expected. The garbage truck was almost full. His hands were stretched forward as if he was diving. Boxes and trash rained down around him as he did a somersault forward into the small mountain of garbage. Carlos and Rebecca slammed into him. Up above them a rectangular hole of sky lit the inside of the truck. The big hydraulic arms lowered the metal dumpster back to the pavement.

"Are you all right?" Rebecca asked. "Is anyone hurt?"

"I'm okay," Carlos said. "We're lucky we didn't hit any glass or nails."

"I think I'm all right." Billy shook his head. "My arm hurts a little. Do you believe it? We actually got dumped!"

Billy looked around the back of the big truck. Off to his left, sitting on top of the rest of the trash by Carlos was the hamster cage. From a quick examination, the cage looked to be in good shape. "It *is* a hamster cage," he said to Carlos and pointed at the contraption of tubes and wires. "This is pretty neat. Can you believe we actually got dumped right out of that big dumpster?"

"This is *not* neat, Billy. How are we going to get out of here?" Rebecca started to stand up to see if she could reach the hole in the roof where they had been dumped, but the big truck began to move backward. She lost her footing and sat down hard. All the children stared at each other silently as the truck moved down the alley to the next dumpster.

"It's picking up another one!" Carlos yelled. "Move to the back or we'll be buried!"

The children scrambled toward the rear of the truck as the hydraulic arms began to whine once more. The rectangle of light in the roof was suddenly blocked out as the next dumpster covered it. Boxes and trash poured in. Then it stopped. The light returned as the big arms lowered the dumpster.

"Yuck!"

"What is it?" Carlos asked.

"I stuck my hand down in something squishy." Rebecca crinkled her nose. She pulled up a crumpled Dairy Queen cup stuffed with a wet chocolate and strawberry napkin.

"He must have been by the Dairy Queen," Carlos said.

"Which is where we should be right now." Rebecca wiped her hand off on some sheets of discarded paper. "I wonder if Josh and Emily and Julie are missing us?"

"Probably," Carlos said.

"I bet they won't guess we're in here," Billy said cheerfully. "Anyone want to bet they won't guess where we are?"

"Of course they won't guess." Rebecca was still trying to clean her hands. "No one would guess we'd be so stupid that we'd get caught in a dumpster and dumped into a garbage truck. What's going to happen to us?"

"He'll probably get the dumpsters in the rest of this alley at least," Carlos said thoughtfully.

"How much trash will he put in here?" Rebecca demanded. "We could get squished."

"I don't know," Carlos said. "I think a lot of garbage trucks can squish the trash so they can put more stuff in each load."

"How do they squish the trash?" Rebecca asked.

"I'm not sure. I think the walls just close in."

"The walls close in?" Rebecca looked around the walls of the truck fearfully. "You're kidding!"

"Nope," Carlos said. "It's run by hydraulics." The truck began to move down the alley. From one dumpster to the next, the huge hydraulic arms emptied the big containers into the back of the truck. The children huddled in the back corner away from the falling debris. After five more dumpsters had been emptied, they could barely see over the mound of trash. The truck rumbled down the alley and came to a stop.

"I think he's done in this alley," Carlos said. "Maybe we'll just—" The boy's words were drowned out by a rumbling, whining sound. The whole truck began to vibrate.

"What's that?" Rebecca yelled.

"We're just moving," Billy said as the trash began to shift beneath his knees.

"We're not just moving! It's the wall!" Rebecca pointed behind her. The back wall of the garbage truck slowly pressed forward in a vibrating whine. The roomful of trash got smaller and smaller.

"Move toward the front!" Carlos yelled as he crawled quickly over the moving trash which began pushing up toward the roof.

"Jesus, help!" Rebecca screamed as the wall came closer. The mound of trash pushed her right up to the roof of the truck. She couldn't go forward because a wooden crate blocked her way and a big heavy sheet of cardboard was pushing against her feet. The whole mound of trash was pushing up. Her head pressed against the roof of the truck.

Then as suddenly as it had begun, it stopped. The rear wall pulled back in the other direction as the mound of trash settled back down. The garbage truck turned out of the alley onto the street. The gears churned as the driver accelerated.

"We're moving," Carlos said.

"Wow! Did you see that wall closing in on us?" Billy asked. "I've never seen anything like it."

"That was too close," Rebecca said with a sigh. Carlos looked around the back of the truck, studying the situation.

"Let's move toward the hole. Maybe we can pull ourselves out through the top and escape."

"I'm for that," Rebecca said. "It smells terrible in here."

"Of course it smells. It's a garbage truck," Billy grunted. "What did you expect?"

"I didn't expect to be stuck in the back of one with the walls closing in," Rebecca shot back. She crawled gingerly over the piles of trash. Her head bumped up against the metal roof. She winced and ducked down.

"Ouch!" Billy yelled. "You stepped on my hand!"

"Don't follow so closely," Rebecca retorted over her shoulder. She pushed a box out of her way and kept moving toward the rectangle of light up ahead. Carlos reached the hole before the others. He grabbed the edge to steady himself and stood up. His head poked out the top. The fresh air blowing on his face felt wonderful. He took several deep breaths.

"We're traveling down Grand Avenue." Carlos ducked back down. "If the truck stops again, I think I can pull myself out and get the driver's attention."

"That would be wonderful." Rebecca slowly stood up, grabbing the edge of the rectangular hole to steady herself. She stuck her head out of the top of the truck and gulped in the air. Billy stood up beside her. Carlos joined his friends. The truck picked up speed as the three children looked out the top.

"Maybe we can yell loud enough when we stop so that someone notices we're in here," Rebecca said as they passed under a traffic signal. Then it happened. The edge of the hole she was holding began to move forward. All three children lost their balance and fell backward.

"The roof is closing!" Billy pointed above them. The rectangle of light was quickly disappearing as the section of roof slid forward.

"We'll suffocate!" Rebecca screamed.

Carlos looked around in the pile of trash. He pulled a piece of wood, a broken chunk of two-by-four, out of the mound. Just as the roof was about to be totally closed off, he stuck the piece of wood through the hole. The sliding roof whined and pinched the piece of lumber, but left a long gap three inches wide in the ceiling above them.

"Good thinking," Billy said to Carlos. Besides letting in air, the gap also let in enough light so the three children could still see, even though the light was much dimmer.

"Thank God," Rebecca said. "I thought we were going to suffocate."

"I doubt if we would have suffocated," Carlos said. "I don't think it's airtight in here, and, besides, there's still lots of space in the trash. There's oxygen all through the trash."

"Not if he dumps more in and keeps squeezing it all tighter and tighter," Rebecca said.

"I don't think he intends to stop," Carlos said. "That's probably why he closed the roof, so trash won't blow out as he goes down the highway."

"We won't be able to get out either," Rebecca said sadly, looking at the slit of light above her. "At least it's quieter now."

"The hamster cage is still in good shape," Billy said, holding it up for the others to see.

"Will you forget that stupid cage!" Rebecca said. "Just because of that cage, we're all trapped like rats."

"That's kind of ironic when you think about it," Carlos said.

"You guys are no fun," Billy said, seeing how serious the others were acting. "We're doing okay. You need to have some faith. God is taking care of us so far, isn't he? If we're stuck in here, we might as well look at the fun side of things."

"The fun side?" Rebecca asked indignantly. "Billy, we're trapped in the back of a garbage truck and no one knows we're in here! Who knows where we'll end up?"

"At the dump," Carlos said.

"What?" Rebecca didn't want to be interrupted while she was lecturing Billy.

"We'll probably end up at the dump," Carlos repeated.

"Yeah," Billy agreed. "We'll get dumped at the dump."

"Dumped?" A new look of fear crossed Rebecca's face. She looked at Carlos. "We're going to get dumped, aren't we?"

"Sure we will," Billy said excitedly.

"But I don't want to get dumped," Rebecca said. "That could be dangerous."

"Quit being such a worry-wart and have a little faith," Billy said. "God has taken care of us so far. We'll be okay, won't we, Carlos?"

"Well . . . I guess it depends how the trash comes out,"

Carlos said. "You could look at it two ways. I imagine everything just dumps out the back. If we crawled to the back of the truck we'd slide out sooner, and we might be able to scoot out of the way before we got buried by a truckload of trash."

"Buried?" Rebecca's voice was rising.

"I could scoot real fast," Billy said confidently. "I wouldn't get buried."

"You don't know that," Rebecca replied irritably. "You've never tried anything like that before."

"You don't know that I couldn't," Billy said. "There's a first time for everything."

"You're impossible," Rebecca said in disgust. She frowned at Billy and turned to Carlos. "What's the other way out?"

"Well, I'm not sure, but I think we could get at the very front of the truck and try to stay on top of all the trash," Carlos added. "That might work, unless . . ."

"Unless what?"

"Unless this container tips like a dump truck. That might cause problems."

"What kind of problems?" Rebecca demanded.

"I don't think you want to know—"

Just then the truck's brakes began to squeal, and all three children were thrown forward. Rebecca reached out to catch a hold of something, anything, but her hands merely grabbed the empty air as she fell over on top of Billy, who was already falling. The squealing tires cried out as the air brakes hissed. The truck finally lurched to a halt. The force of the stop jarred the top sliding panel open wider, and the two-by-four that Carlos had stuck in the crack fell, almost hitting Billy in the head.

Then everything was quiet.

"Is everyone okay?" Rebecca asked anxiously.

"I think so," Carlos replied, rubbing his arm. He had put his arm out to catch himself and had scraped it on the edge of a cardboard box.

"I'm all right," Billy said. "That board almost clobbered me when it fell out of the roof."

They looked at the board and then up at the gap in the roof. The truck began to move again. The children all sat up and tried to make themselves comfortable.

"I don't think the driver hit anything," Rebecca said.

"I guess not," Carlos replied. "I wonder why he stopped so fast."

"Maybe he was scared of hitting a dog," Billy said. "Our dad did that once out on Highway 17. A big old farm dog ran out of the woods in front of him, and he hit the brakes suddenly. We swerved all over the place because it had just started to rain and it was wet."

"Dad missed the dog, fortunately," Rebecca remembered.

The truck picked up speed. The engine rumbled as the driver changed gears. Carlos looked up at the slot of sky through the crack in the sliding roof. He picked up the board. "You know, we better stick that board up in there before—"

The children were all looking up as the sliding roof whined and suddenly began to slide shut. Carlos quickly picked up the board and poked it up at the roof, but he hit solid metal as the roof shut tight. The children were covered in darkness as the big garbage truck rolled down the road.

Chapter Four

The Man with the Red Beard

The man with the red beard and sunglasses grabbed Emily's wrist with one hand and reached out with his other hand. He plucked the small dark object out of her hand.

"Hey, let her alone!" Josh said angrily.

"This doesn't belong to you, does it?" the man said, examining the object intently. He ignored Josh's comment. He took off his sunglasses. He looked older with the sunglasses off since it showed the wrinkles around his hard gray eyes.

"I found it," Emily said uneasily. "So you're right, it doesn't really belong to me."

"Where did you find it?" the man demanded.

"Down the alley behind the shoestore," Emily replied.

"What's going on?" Josh demanded. He didn't like being treated as if his opinion about things didn't matter.

"Show me where you found it," the man said, ignoring Josh.

"Right down here." Emily walked down the alley. As they began walking, a blue car pulled up behind them. The driver followed them down the alley. Josh glanced back. The man was staring right at them, no expression showing on his face.

"I found it right here." Emily pointed to the ground.

"You found it here, and not in the dumpster over there?" the man asked seriously.

"It was lying on the pavement," Emily replied.

"What's going on?" Josh demanded. "What did you find?"

"A computer chip," Emily said. "I think it's a microprocessor."

"A microprocessor?" Julie asked. "What kind of chip is that?"

"A real expensive one," Emily said. "It's a Z-5000, one of the new upgrades for personal computers. The Z-5000 is one of the fastest upgrade chips on the market."

"*The* fastest on the market," the man said with a thin smile. "A real hot seller. Worth about five hundred dollars a pop."

"What do you mean *upgrade*?" Julie asked.

"Instead of buying a whole new computer, you can replace your old microprocessor chip with the Z-5000 and your computer will run ten times faster."

"Twenty times faster in most cases," the man said. "They're brand new, the best on the market."

"Then why did you find it lying in the alley?" Josh asked. "What's going on here?"

"Your little friend found an important item," the man said

and smiled, showing his yellow teeth. "You see, I was here unloading a computer for the shoestore this afternoon, and we lost this. I'm really glad you found it. It could have been crushed or something just lying there on the pavement like that."

"How did you lose it?" Emily asked carefully.

"We were installing the new computer, and I guess it fell out of the box when we were carrying it in," the man said. "I can't tell you how glad I am to get it back. We thought maybe we lost it in the computer box and that it got thrown into the dumpster by mistake. I thought we were going to have to go buy another upgrade chip."

"You weren't able to do the upgrade then since you only had that chip?" Emily asked.

"Yeah, it was a shame," the man said. "We wasted over an hour looking around. Now I'll have to test this chip to make sure it still works before we can do the upgrade."

"That's too bad," Josh said. "When you were here earlier, you didn't happen to see some other kids in the alley, did you?"

"Other kids? What did they look like?"

"Rebecca and Billy are African-American," Julie said. "And Carlos is Hispanic."

"We didn't see anyone like that," the man said and shrugged.

"We found their bikes here, but we can't find them," Josh said. "They were here about an hour ago, I imagine."

"Three kids, huh?" the man said. He shook his head. "Thanks for finding my computer chip. I hope it still works. And just to show you how grateful we are, I want to give you a little token of my appreciation."

The man reached into his front pocket. He pulled out a silver clip filled with folded green bills. He took a bill from the pack and gave it to Emily.

"Twenty dollars!" Emily frowned. "I can't take this." She tried to hand the money back to the man.

The man stepped back and shook his head. "It's yours as a little reward. You saved me a lot more money than that. You kids take it easy now."

The man turned and got into the waiting blue car. The children moved out of the way as the car moved slowly down the alley.

"Twenty dollars!" Josh said. "You really hit the jackpot."

"Get the license plate number on that car!" Emily whispered.

"What?" Josh asked.

" 'EL 6592,' " Emily said out loud. She pulled a pen from her pocket and wrote it quickly on the palm of her hand. The car turned out of the alley and onto the street.

"What are you doing that for?" Josh asked.

"That man was lying," Emily replied.

"Lying about what?" Julie asked.

"He was lying about the chip and who knows what else," Emily said fiercely. "I don't think he was installing a computer in the shoestore this afternoon."

"Why not?"

"Because he lied about having only one chip," Emily said angrily. "The whole story is probably a lie. Let's go ask Mr. Warren if those guys really sold him a computer."

"Why are you so upset? The man gave you twenty dollars. Did you want more?"

"Of course not," Emily said.

"Then how are you so sure he was lying to you?"

"Because I didn't just find one chip," Emily said. She dug into her front pocket. She carefully pulled out three other Z-5000 chips. "I found four of these, not just the one. But he said he only lost one."

"Maybe he was mistaken," Julie offered.

"He wouldn't make a mistake about chips as expensive as these," Emily said. "Four of them are worth $2000."

"I think you're right," Josh agreed, staring at the three microprocessors. "Something strange is going on here."

"I think we should go talk to Mr. Warren in the shoestore just to make sure," Emily said. "If he never heard of that guy, then we better go see Sheriff Weaver right away."

"What about Carlos and Billy and Rebecca?" Julie asked.

"Maybe they know something about these chips," Emily said. "Maybe that guy was in the alley earlier, and he lied about not seeing them. He could be lying about everything."

"That's right," Josh said seriously. "They wouldn't just leave their bicycles here like that."

"Do you think that guy could have kidnapped them?" Julie asked. The other children were quiet, not wanting to think about it.

"Let's not jump to conclusions," Josh tried to reassure the others. "Just because that guy might be lying about the chips doesn't mean he's a kidnapper. He wouldn't have any reason to kidnap them."

"But what's going on then?" Emily asked her brother.

"I don't know," Josh said helplessly. "Let's go talk to Mr. Warren in the shoestore and check out that guy's story. He may have lost more chips and just didn't want you to know it."

"I'm sure he was lying," Emily said with determination.

"You may be right," Julie said. "He did seem a little nervous to me."

"I don't think we should jump to conclusions," Josh replied. "You can't make judgments without knowing all the facts. Let's go check out his story."

The three children rode their bicycles down the alley and up to the front of the shoestore. They walked in quickly. A young man was arranging cans of shoe polish on the racks.

"That's not Mr. Warren," Emily said.

"Hi," the young man said. "Can I help you all? We've got a sale on athletic shoes this week. Look at these Nikes." He held up a pair of shoes and handed them to Josh. Josh looked at the shoes briefly. He liked the way new athletic shoes looked, so fresh and clean, and they smelled good. He smiled and handed the shoes back.

"That's not really why we're here," Josh said.

"Oh?"

"We were hoping to talk to Mr. Warren," Emily said.

"He's not here today. But maybe I could help you."

"We wanted to know if he was getting an upgrade to his computer today," Emily quickly said.

"Computer upgrade?" The young man smiled. "We don't even have a computer."

"You don't?" Julie asked.

"How can you do business without a computer?"

"Mr. Warren doesn't. Says he doesn't need one. I've been working for him for three months. He's kind of old fashioned, I guess. He keeps his own books, on paper, and has his own system of keeping track of shoes. He said he's been doing it that way for forty years, and he doesn't need to change now."

"Well, do you know if a computer salesman was here recently trying to sell him a new computer?" Josh asked. "Maybe Mr. Warren decided to buy one."

"No way," the young man said. "I would have heard about it. No one has been here trying to sell computers in the last three months anyway."

"That's odd," Josh said.

"Not if you knew Mr. Warren. Like I said, he's old fashioned. He's just got no use for computers."

"Was there a man with a short red beard in here earlier today?" Emily asked.

"Nope."

"Are you sure?" Josh asked.

"Hey, look. This isn't a department store. I remember all my customers. I haven't had anyone with a red beard, black beard or blue beard in here today. No beards at all."

"Let's go," Emily said. "I think we have our answer."

"Answer to what?" the young man asked.

"We met someone with a red beard in the alley who said he was here today trying to upgrade Mr. Warren's computer with a new microprocessor," Emily said.

"That *is* strange because it sure didn't happen," the young man said with a puzzled look on his face. "My name is Rob Baker, by the way. You guys look familiar somehow. What're your names?"

The children introduced themselves. Rob's face lit up. "You guys are the ones they call the Home School Detectives, aren't you? I've read about you all in the newspaper."

"Mrs. Highsmith has written nice things," Josh replied. "Well, thanks for your help. We'd better go. Our friends are missing."

"Missing?" Rob asked.

Josh quickly told him about the events of the morning which led up to their finding the bikes in the alley and meeting the man with the red beard. Rob listened intently.

"So then we came in here to check out the story of the guy with the red beard," Josh said. "It seems for sure he was lying, but I don't know why. And we still don't know where to look for our friends."

"These are what the microprocessors look like." Emily pulled one out of her pocket. "They're worth a lot of money."

"What's that big *W* on there mean?" Rob looked closely at the chip. "I don't know much about computer chips."

"It stands for Worthington Industries," Emily said. "This chip is one of the best upgrades on the market."

"Worthington has a big factory over in Round Rock, don't they?" Rob asked. "My older brother used to work there."

Just then, the door to the shoestore opened and a tall woman with three little boys came in. Rob waved at her. She began looking at a long rack filled with children's shoes.

"I'll need to go help that customer," Rob said.

"We need to go look for Billy and the others," Josh said anxiously.

"Have you looked in the other stores on this block?" Rob asked with helpful concern. "Maybe they're shopping or looking."

"That's probably the best thing to do first," Josh said.

"But I want to check in the alley by the dumpster first," Emily said. "There might have been another one of these chips off to the side of the alley that I missed the first time."

"You can go through the back of the store if you like," Rob said helpfully. "You just follow that hallway out to the back door. That will save you some time."

"Thanks," Emily said.

"Good luck in finding your friends." Rob then turned and walked over to the woman with the three children.

Emily led the way to the back of the shoestore with Josh and Julie following reluctantly. They walked past big shelves filled with boxes and boxes of shoes. Emily walked with determination to the rear door that led into the alley. She pushed the door open with force.

The sun was bright. Emily walked quickly across the alley. She looked carefully on the ground where she found the chips. Then she looked down near the bottom of the dumpster.

"Come on, we need to get going," Josh said impatiently.

"I don't see any more," Emily said sadly. "At least I don't feel bad holding onto the other chips I found, now that I know that guy was lying. I could actually use these in my own computer. I'll have to ask Mom and Dad if I should keep them, of course. But I know the guy wasn't telling the truth, so I don't think they belong to him. Maybe I could even sell the other two chips. Lots of families in the home school co-op would like to upgrade. It would make all the software run quicker, especially the CD-ROM multimedia programs. But maybe we should go to Sheriff Weaver first and tell them about that guy and the way he lied to us. Maybe he's not really—"

Emily looked up at Josh. She was surprised at the expression on his and Julie's faces. Both of them seemed scared. They were looking in her direction, but not at her.

"What's wrong with you guys?" Emily asked. She heard a noise behind her. She whirled around. The man with the red beard was standing behind the dumpster looking at her with a smile. He seemed especially glad that she was holding another chip.

"I think you have something that belongs to me," the man said evenly.

"I don't know that these belong to you." Emily's voice cracked. Part of her felt frightened by the man's sudden appearance and part of her was just plain angry. "You lied about doing an upgrade on the shoestore computer. We were just in there and they don't even have a computer."

"Is that so?" the man said. "I guess I was confused."

"What's going on?" Josh demanded. "Why were you hiding behind the dumpster like that?"

"I wasn't hiding," the man said. "You just didn't see me."

"We better be going, you guys," Julie said nervously. "We still need to find Billy and the others."

"No one is going anywhere yet," the man with the red beard said. He waved his arm. Down the alley, the blue sedan began to move toward them.

"Hey, mister, we don't want any trouble," Josh said quickly. "My sister will give you back your computer chips."

"I will not. I don't think he owns them."

"Just give them back," Josh whispered as the blue car drew alongside the children.

"I don't just want the chips," the man with the red beard said with a crooked smile. "I think you children and I need to have a nice long talk."

"I think we should all go down and talk with Sheriff Weaver if you want these chips back," Emily replied hotly.

"I don't think we need to do that," the man said. "I think we just need to take a little ride and talk. That's all."

"I'm not going anywhere with you!" Emily said. The man

smiled and slowly pulled a small revolver out his pocket. He pointed it at Emily.

"I think you all need to just calm down and come with me," the man said firmly. He opened the car door and motioned for them to get inside.

Chapter Five

To the Dump

The garbage truck rumbled along the road. Billy, Rebecca and Carlos huddled together in the darkness in the back of the truck, trying to make themselves comfortable.

"It stinks in here," Rebecca said.

"That's about the one-hundredth time you've said that," Billy replied. "We all know it stinks."

"Well, we shouldn't be in here. This is all your fault."

"Not exactly," Billy said defensively. "I was just trying to get the hamster cage and then that big bee showed up. Carlos and I fell into the dumpster. You were the one who jumped in."

"I should have just gone to the Dairy Queen with the others," Rebecca moaned. "I could have gotten the computer game tomorrow or later."

"Things could be worse," Billy said.

"How?"

"Well, he's not dumping any more trash on us," Billy said. "And we aren't really hurt. The walls didn't close in and crush us."

"What about when he dumps us out?" Rebecca asked. "We could get buried alive."

"I don't think that will happen," Billy said. "You have to have faith. In fact, I've been praying we'll get dumped without a scratch."

"I haven't heard you praying," Rebecca retorted.

"I've been praying silently," Billy replied. "I didn't want you to think I was worried or anything."

"Well, I'm worried. I'm worried plenty."

"We'll have our chance to find out what's going to happen pretty soon," Carlos said abruptly.

"How do you know?" Billy asked.

"Because the truck is slowing down," Rebecca answered nervously.

The gears whined and the air brakes hissed briefly as the garbage truck slowed and began to turn. The children reached out and tried to brace themselves as the truck began riding along a bumpy road.

"I bet we're at a landfill," Carlos said.

"He's really going to dump us," Rebecca whimpered.

"He doesn't know we're in here," Billy said. "It's nothing personal."

"It's personal to me!" Rebecca replied. "It's my person, my body that's going to get dumped like it's an old broken chair. Oooohhh, I hope we don't get hurt."

The truck suddenly stopped. The children immediately began yelling for help. But almost as soon as they did, the truck began moving again.

"He's backing up, I think," Carlos yelled to the others. "Climb toward the front of the truck. That's our best chance to stay on top of the trash as it falls out."

The three children crawled awkwardly toward the front of the truck. Billy stopped when he touched the front wall.

"Just keep praying," Billy yelled to the others. "God will get us out of here."

"Oh, Lord, help us!" Rebecca moaned.

The big truck hissed to a stop. Almost immediately a whining noise filled the air as the hydraulic pistons began to tip up the back of the truck. All the children screamed when the rear door of the truck suddenly opened up. Light flashed into their eyes, blinding them as the trash began falling. Billy reached out and grabbed Rebecca's arm, and Carlos grabbed Billy's leg.

The trash slid out the rear of the truck as one long mound. The truck moved slowly forward as the trash fell, making a longer but lower pile rather than a big heap. Rebecca screamed as she slid out the rear of the truck, but it wasn't as far a drop as she anticipated since she was on top of the heap of trash. Billy and Carlos fell in a tangle of arms and legs beside her. The dust in the load of trash was perhaps the worst thing. All the children were coughing and waving their arms in front of their faces, trying to clear the air.

"He's not . . . not stopping!" Rebecca coughed, pointing at the truck, which was rapidly gaining speed as it rolled away, out of the landfill area.

"Wait!" Carlos yelled out. But the truck just kept clanking along as it rolled over the bumpy dirt road that led away from the dump. The load from the garbage truck sat in front of a huge mountain of trash over fifty yards wide. Several other single loads of garbage were lying in front of the big wall of trash, waiting to be pushed into the big trash mountain.

"Is anyone hurt?" Rebecca asked, struggling to get down off the mound of trash.

"Not me," Carlos said, wiping the dust off his arms.

"Me neither," Billy added. "That wasn't even scary. The kiddy rides at a carnival are a lot more scary than that."

"Well, it could have been a lot worse," Rebecca chided.

"But God took care of us, didn't he?" Billy replied. "You just have to have some faith. Now where's that hamster cage?"

Billy began searching in the trash. Rebecca looked at her curious brother and shook her head in amazement. Carlos smiled.

"I found it!" Billy said with glee. He reached down under a big cardboard box and lifted up the hamster cage. He held up the cage as if it were a prized possession. Then something else caught his eye. "Those striped boxes!"

Billy set the cage aside and pulled out two red-and-blue-striped boxes from the pile of trash. He bent down to lift them up. "These weigh a lot. Come help me, Carlos." The two boys dragged the boxes off the mound of trash to the bare dirt.

"What are you guys messing with now?" Rebecca demanded. "We need to get out of here."

"These are those boxes that guy in the limousine dumped, remember?" Billy asked. The boxes were taped shut. Billy took out his pocketknife and cut the tape on one.

"Wow!" Billy lifted off the lid. Then his face became puzzled as he stared down in the box. "What are they?"

"Some kind of computer chips," Carlos said.

"Where's the rest of the computer?" Billy asked, plainly disappointed.

"These are just chips," Carlos said, picking one up. "They look brand new, but it's hard to tell. See that big *W*? That means they're made by Worthington Industries."

"But there's no computer," Billy said. "Wait. There's a plastic envelope in this one." Billy pulled a small plastic envelope about the size of a sandwich bag out of the box.

"What's that?" Carlos asked.

"There's a piece of paper and a key," Billy said. "The paper says, 'D-19.' And there's a time written down: 'nine-thirty.' And there's a map of Springdale with a red circle."

"That could be some kind of message," Carlos said excitedly. "I bet there's something important in Springdale where it's circled."

"Well, I found it first," Billy replied, putting the paper and key back into the plastic bag. He stuffed the bag into the rear pocket on his jeans.

"Let's see if there's any more stuff in here." Carlos quickly looked through the box. "Nope. Just computer chips. But there sure are a lot of them. I bet these are worth a lot of money."

"Then why would someone put them in the trash?" Rebecca asked.

"You saw the way those two men were acting, didn't you?" Carlos said. "That man in the limousine looked like he was hiding the chips in the dumpster, not throwing them away."

"Maybe. I think you guys have just seen too many cops-and-robbers shows on television," Rebecca said skeptically.

"It could be robbers," Carlos insisted. "Why would people meet in an alley like that unless something sneaky was going on? Don't you remember how fast they took off down the alley when they left?"

"I thought it was suspicious," Billy said, but he was rapidly losing interest in the computer chips when there was a whole dump to explore. He began to walk away from the others.

"Where are you going?" Rebecca demanded.

"I'm going to see if anyone is over by the bulldozer." Billy walked beyond the loads of garbage. "Then I want to look around."

"Don't mess with any knobs or keys or anything!" Billy nodded, but Rebecca wasn't convinced he was listening.

"They wouldn't leave a key in a bulldozer," Carlos said, trying to reassure Rebecca. Then he began to wonder. He watched Billy run toward the bulldozer.

"What do you think we should do, Carlos?" Rebecca asked.

"I think these boxes would be too heavy for us to carry out of here. Maybe if we found an old wagon or—"

"Forget the boxes! How are we going to get home? We don't even know where we are!"

"We're at the county landfill, I assume," Carlos said. "It's closer to Round Rock than to Springdale, I think."

"But how—"

Just then the children saw an approaching vehicle raising up a cloud of dust. The dust cloud was moving rapidly toward them.

"Good, someone's coming," Rebecca said.

"It's a pickup truck," Carlos said, squinting his eyes. "You know, it looks just like that pickup truck we saw in the alley with Mr. Cowboy Hat."

"It does look familiar," Rebecca said.

The red pickup rolled up to the mound of trash. A blue tarp covered the bed of the truck. A tall man with a cowboy hat and mustache got out. A large, heavy-set Asian man got out of the passenger side of the truck.

"What are you kids doing here?" the man with the cowboy hat asked.

"We got trapped in a dumpster and got dumped," Rebecca said. "We're sure glad to see you."

"We're looking for something that got dumped by mistake too," the man with the cowboy hat said with a crooked smile.

"I bet you're looking for these boxes," Rebecca said, pointing to the red-and-blue-striped boxes. "They're full of computer chips."

"Now how did you know that?" the man said with a big smile.

"We saw you in the alley behind the toystore," Rebecca said cheerfully. "You know, when you stopped to talk to that guy in the limousine?"

The man with the cowboy hat looked at the Asian man. The Asian man frowned. Carlos, seeing the look passed between the two men, began to feel worried.

"Just what did you see?" Mr. Cowboy Hat asked.

"Nothing, really," Carlos said.

"What do you mean, Carlos?" Rebecca asked. "We saw the whole thing. The man in the limousine put the boxes in the dumpster before you got there. Then you two were arguing . . . and . . ."

Rebecca suddenly got quiet when she realized Carlos was silently motioning her to shut up. The two men seemed very interested in hearing what Rebecca had to say.

"Sounds like these kids were spying on us, doesn't it,

Chan?" Mr. Cowboy Hat said.

"We weren't spying." Rebecca's voice cracked. "We were just trapped and—"

"I think you kids better come with us," the man with the cowboy hat said.

"Run!" Carlos yelled at Rebecca. Rebecca ran past the pickup truck down the makeshift dirt road as Carlos headed toward the mountain of trash. The Asian man quickly ran after Rebecca. In the open spaces she was no match for the grown man. He ran her down and grabbed her arm. She jerked and pulled, but his fingers felt like steel. She screamed, but he only smiled and laughed at her feeble struggles.

Carlos could hear Rebecca screaming, but he was afraid to look back. Mr. Cowboy Hat was right behind him. Carlos started climbing up the mountain of trash. The big man slowed down to climb. Carlos reached for a broken wheel of a baby carriage when his feet slipped on a plastic garbage bag. The boy and bag rolled down the hill, right into the man's legs.

"Gotcha!" the man hissed as he grabbed Carlos by the back of the neck. He pinched down hard.

"Ouch!" Carlos winced.

The man dragged Carlos off the pile of trash. When they got back to the pickup truck, Chan was already tying Rebecca's arms and legs with a roll of heavy twine.

She was wiggling wildly, but it didn't do any good. The more she wiggled, the tighter the Asian man pulled the knots.

"Tie 'em up and I'll get the boxes," Mr. Cowboy Hat said. He shoved Carlos toward Chan. "We'll go back to the mansion and see what we're supposed to do next."

Carlos struggled. He tried to look over at the bulldozer, wondering if Billy had seen them trying to escape. But Billy was nowhere in sight. Chan smiled as he began tying the knots.

"Put 'em up front with us," Mr. Cowboy Hat said. Chan managed to carry a wiggling Rebecca into the front seat first. Then he started on Carlos. When the man's grip loosened, Carlos tore free and began running down the road in front of the pickup truck toward the entrance of the landfill.

"Help! Help! Help!" Carlos yelled. But having his arms tied put him off balance, so he couldn't run very fast. Mr. Cowboy Hat was laughing as he chased him.

"Like trying to rope a young steer, ain't it, Chan?" Mr. Cowboy Hat said. The other man leered and joined the chase.

Billy, who had been watching from behind the bulldozer ever since the two men arrived, saw his chance. He darted from behind the bulldozer and ran for the pickup while watching the two the whole time. He reached the back of the truck without being seen. He lifted up the blue tarp and quickly climbed in.

Mr. Cowboy Hat caught Carlos first. Both men grabbed Carlos's arms and escorted him back to the truck. Chan held Carlos while Mr. Cowboy Hat walked over to the pile of trash and picked up the two red-and-blue-striped boxes. He carried them to the rear of the pickup truck. He lifted up the edge of the tarp and put the boxes in the back of the truck.

Mr. Cowboy Hat smiled as he walked to the front of the truck. Carlos tried to jerk his arms free one final time, but the two men had no trouble holding the boy. They pushed Carlos onto the seat beside Rebecca. Then the men got in on either side of the children. Mr. Cowboy Hat started the pickup. He drove off quickly, leaving a trail of dust that slowly drifted over the mounds of trash.

Chapter Six

Partners in Crime

Rob Baker, the shoe clerk, sold Mrs. Carson six pairs of shoes. He was holding the door open for her to leave when he saw the three bicycles parked in front of the store. Seeing them, he remembered Josh, Emily and Julie. They had been gone a long time. He walked to the back of the store and opened the door to the alley.

The alley appeared to be empty. Rob scratched his head. Down behind the toystore, he saw three other bicycles parked by the wall.

"Those are their friends' bikes," Rob said to himself. "Anyone out here?" he called. He looked behind the garbage dumpster. He scratched his head again and went inside. He thought about their story about the man with the red beard and the computer chips. He felt a nagging sense of worry.

"I wonder if I should call Mr. Warren and tell him about the children," he mumbled to himself as he put away the extra shoes that Mrs. Carson didn't buy. The front doorbell rang and an old man walked in.

"Be there in a second!" Rob called out. He quickly put away another shoebox. "Those kids are probably looking for their friends in the stores on this block like I suggested. I guess they're all right."

He pushed the nagging sense of worry out of his mind and walked over to help the old man.

The blue sedan backed up in front of a door. The man with the red beard led the three blindfolded children across the gravel driveway. He opened a black metal door and led them inside a hall.

"Just keep walking," the man said.

"What are you going to do with us?" Josh demanded. Being blindfolded was scary, but he was equally angry at being held captive.

"You're going to be okay," the man replied. "Like I told you in the car, we're trying to bust up a possible theft ring, and you kids just got into the middle of it."

"Then why don't you take us to the police?" Emily asked. "Sheriff Weaver is a friend of ours. If somebody is stealing something, he'd help you."

"He may be part of the whole scheme and not to be trusted," the man said. "I've told you all of this before. You kids are safer here."

"Then why the blindfolds? What are you afraid we'll see?" Julie retorted angrily.

"I'm sorry about the blindfolds, but it's for your own good," the man said patiently. "Once this is all over, you'll probably get some kind of reward."

"I bet," Josh said.

The man led them into a small room with some folding chairs and a table. He unfolded three of the chairs and had the children sit down. After they were sitting, he untied the blindfolds, starting with Julie, then Emily and finally Josh.

"You kids just sit tight and don't make any trouble," the man warned. "I've had a long day, and I don't need any hassles. I have a friend who will be here soon, and he's going to talk to you. You just tell him the truth. No lies. Mr. Chan is not a man who likes any trouble. And once you finish talking to him, we'll probably let you go."

"You better," Josh said. "You're going to be sorry you ever took us."

"Yeah, right." The man with the red beard smiled. He walked out of the room and closed the door. They all heard him putting a key into the door and the lock click. As soon as he was gone, Josh sprang up from his chair and immediately tried the doorknob. "It's locked." Josh turned the knob again. He pushed against the door and then pulled. The door wouldn't budge.

"You probably shouldn't try to get out." Emily sniffled. "What are we going to do?"

Julie leaned over and patted Emily on the back. Josh left the door and sat down by his sister. He propped his elbows on the long table and began to think.

"If only I hadn't picked up those computer chips," Emily said.

"You couldn't know what was going to happen," Josh said. "All I can figure is that we've gotten caught in the middle of some crime related to those computer chips."

"Maybe they're not really microprocessors at all," Emily

said slowly. "Maybe they're some kind of ROM chip with secret information encoded in them. I saw a movie once where these spies hid secret information inside a video-game cartridge. You can store a ton of codes and things inside a chip the size of those Z-5000s. Maybe it's something like that. Those guys could be some kind of spies."

"But why would they leave computer chips with secret information inside them lying right on the alley pavement?" Julie asked. "That doesn't make sense."

"Red Beard acted like they should have been in the dumpster," Josh said. "There must have been some kind of mix-up or mistake. And he obviously thinks that we know more than we're saying or else he wouldn't have brought us here."

The children heard footsteps in the hall. Josh stiffened when the door opened. The man with the red beard came in, followed by a heavyset Asian man.

"This is Mr. Chan," the man with the red beard said. "He doesn't speak the best of English. He's new to the country, but I'm sure smart children like you will understand what he wants."

"More children?" the big man grunted. He had a thick accent. He frowned so hard his heavy, dark eyebrows seemed to touch each other.

"What do you mean, 'More children'?" the man with the red beard asked with alarm.

"You tell me. We find two children at dump with the boxes. They saw us in the alley, so we bring them back. We bring back the boxes, only there is no key and no map. Mr. Wu is very upset. Now you bring children here also. Mr. Wu may think you have other partners that you are not telling us about."

"Other partners? You think these kids are my partners? Don't be absurd. That's an absolutely crazy idea. I never saw these kids before today. You can ask Carl if you want. He was driving the car."

"Mr. Wu is not man to double-cross."

"I'm not trying to double-cross anyone."

"Then why all these kids?" Chan demanded. "Everywhere we go, kids and more kids!"

"I was just trying to tie up loose ends. I swear that's all I was doing."

"Hmmmmm." Chan stared at Josh. "You know this man?"

"No way. I never even saw him before today, and I regret that we ever met."

"What did you do with map and key?" Chan looked from child to child.

"We don't know what you're talking about," Emily said. "We were just in the alley looking for our friends."

"Then how did you get these chips?" Chan asked, holding out the four Z-5000 chips in his hand.

"I found them in the alley," Emily said. "That's all. They were lying on the pavement."

Mr. Chan grunted. He frowned at the children in silence. He looked at the man with the red beard with suspicion. Then he smiled as he thought of something. "You know little black girl name of Rebecca?"

Josh, Emily and Julie all looked at each other in surprise. Mr. Chan watched them carefully.

"You do know such a girl?" the big man asked again.

"We have a friend named Rebecca," Josh said cautiously. "She's African-American."

"How old this girl?" Chan demanded.

"She's ten years old," Emily said. "What's going on? She and her brother, Billy, are twins. Have you seen them?"

"Brother?" Chan asked curiously. "Her brother not a Mexican boy named Carlos?"

"You've seen Carlos?" Julie asked.

"You know boy named Carlos?" Chan responded with surprise.

"I have an adopted brother named Carlos," Julie said. "He's Hispanic."

"Your brother?" Mr. Chan said and smiled broadly. He looked suspiciously at the man with the red beard.

"Now wait a minute," Red Beard said quickly. "I tell you I never saw these kids before today. You can't think I'd really have them as some kind of partners? The whole idea is just crazy."

"Then how come these kids know each other?"

"I don't know. Maybe they don't," Red Beard said. "Maybe they're lying. How would I know? We don't know that they know each other. Maybe it's a coincidence . . . or maybe—"

"Mr. Wu not like this situation," Chan said tersely. "Everything becoming very, very messy."

"Well, I can assure you, I've been holding up my end of the bargain," Red Beard said. "I'm taking all the risk here, after all. Surely Mr. Wu can appreciate all the problems I've—"

"Outside." Chan nodded toward the door. The two men walked outside. The door lock clicked. Josh ran over to the door. The two men were arguing in the hall. Josh stuck his ear against the door to listen.

"Mr. Wu not like children involved," Chan accused. "Why

are they here if not friends of yours?"

"I told you, I couldn't take a chance," Red Beard replied. "I didn't know what they knew. Besides, they were snooping around too much in the alley. The girl had some of the chips. I was afraid they'd go to the police, and who knows what would happen?"

"Why do they know the children we found at the dump?" Chan demanded.

"How would I know?"

"Both girl and boy had been looking into the boxes at dump," Chan said. "But the key and map were not there."

"What did you do with the children?" Red Beard asked.

"Why are you so interested?" Chan asked suspiciously. "Maybe these children *are* working for you. Maybe you and your cousin both trying to cheat Mr. Wu."

"I tell you I don't know *any* of these children," Red Beard insisted shrilly. "I just wanted to know what you did with the children you found."

"They're in safe place," Chan grunted. "Once the shipment leaves the country, they are of no concern."

"I don't like this," Red Beard replied. "None of this is working out like you guys said it would. I hope you're not trying to double-cross me, because if you are I'll—"

"Mr. Wu not double-crosser." Chan cut him off. "Your cousin is one who messed things up. He's trying to cheat Mr. Wu, and he will pay dearly for it. He said map and key were in boxes."

Just then, other voices filled the hallway. Red Beard and Chan walked away from the door. Josh pressed his ear harder against the wall.

"What's going on?" Emily asked.

"I can't hear any more," Josh said. He frowned and walked down the wall to the corner of the room. He pressed his ear against the wall and listened. He could hear people talking, but he couldn't make out the words.

"Can you hear now?" Julie asked. Josh shook his head sadly.

"Not clear enough," Josh replied. He quickly told the others what he had heard while at the door.

"Red Beard is getting nervous and scared, it seems to me," Julie said.

"I think you're right," Josh replied. "They were supposed to get a map and key in some boxes that apparently got thrown into the dumpster behind the shoestore. That big guy Chan thinks Red Beard may be trying to double-cross him, and Red Beard thinks that he's the one being double-crossed."

"There's no honor among thieves," Julie observed.

"It doesn't sound like it," Josh said.

"Do you think they actually found Rebecca and Carlos at the dump?" Emily asked.

"That's what it sounded like to me," Josh said, shaking his head. "But don't ask me how that could happen."

"But what about Billy?" Julie asked.

"Yeah, what about Billy?" Emily asked.

"I don't know," Josh replied, shrugging his shoulders.

There were footsteps in the hall. The door opened quickly. Mr. Chan and Red Beard came back inside. Red Beard's face was flushed. He looked very nervous.

"You say black girl has a twin brother?" Chan asked Josh.

"Yes," Josh said slowly.

"Where is this brother?"

"I don't know," Josh said honestly. "We were looking for

them at the toystore earlier. The last I knew, he was with Carlos and Rebecca."

Mr. Chan paused to think. Then he smiled. He turned toward the man with the red beard. "We need find this boy now!" The big man left the room quickly. Red Beard followed, locking the door behind him.

Chapter Seven

Under Cover

Whe**n** Billy climbed into the back of the pickup at the dump, he discovered several large metal trunks under the tarp. All the lids were closed, and they were locked with padlocks. He wasn't sure what to do, so he prayed quickly, feeling both excited and afraid. He knew he could be discovered at any instant. Then he had an idea. He wiggled his way among the trunks and wedged himself between them and the front of the pickup truck. Just then, he heard the men outside the truck talking as they brought Carlos back. Billy scrunched down as low as he could. He saw a flash of light as Mr. Cowboy Hat put the two boxes of computer chips into the back of the truck. Then he lowered the tarp, and the truck took off.

Billy wanted more than anything to look out from under the tarp, but he was afraid that one of the men might see him peeking. In the dim light in the back of the truck, he lit the dial on his watch to check the time. It was only 1:30 in the afternoon. He felt hungry for lunch and for the ice cream cone he'd missed at the Dairy Queen.

The truck bounced along the dump road and then turned. The ride became less bumpy and the boy knew they were on a paved road, going somewhere. But where? he wondered. He could hear voices in the cab in front of him, but he couldn't make out any words.

"This is my second unexpected ride of the day," the boy thought. "At least it isn't as smelly as the garbage truck."

He hoped Carlos and Rebecca were doing okay. He didn't hear any screams. But knowing Rebecca, she would be plenty scared. Billy hoped she wasn't too frightened. Even though he and she had disagreements and occasional fights, there was never any question that he really did love his sister. The more he thought about it, the angrier he felt toward the two men who had tied her up.

The truck slowed down. Billy checked his watch when they stopped. The ride lasted almost thirty minutes. Billy moved to the side of the truck and carefully lifted the edge of the tarp. He thought they would be returning to Springdale, but he was wrong. They started moving again and passed over some railroad tracks. Then the truck turned down a long, tree-lined lane.

The truck slowed down once more. Billy saw a gate attached to a large brick buttress. A massive stone lion sat on top of the buttress. The truck drove up a long, winding driveway. In the distance Billy could see a huge mansion.

"What a house!" he whispered to himself. But the truck didn't stop. It passed the house and kept going. Everything got darker as the truck pulled into some kind of garage. The truck doors opened and slammed shut. Billy thought about jumping out when they stopped and trying to attack the two men. Part of him wanted to try, but he knew a small boy against two grown men wouldn't be much of a challenge.

"I need to stay free so I can go get help," Billy reasoned.

"You kids come with Chan," a voice said harshly. "No funny business."

Billy scrunched down behind a metal trunk just in time. He held his breath tensely. The rear of the tarp was lifted up. He could hear someone grunt. He figured that someone was taking out the two striped boxes.

Billy heard a low heavy rumble in the distance, then everything was quiet. He waited, not sure what to do. He waited five minutes. Then ten. By then he figured that he was safe.

He lifted up the edge of the tarp slowly. He expected to find himself in a garage. He lifted the tarp higher, cautiously looking around. The room was quite dark. He then realized he was in a kind of barn. He stuck his head out of the tarp slowly. Seeing no one, he climbed over the side of the pickup truck and hopped down.

Billy looked around curiously. He had never been in such a huge barn. It was long and low and dark. Light came from underneath a crack in a long wooden door. Billy walked toward the light. On the dirt floor he could see truck tracks. The long wooden door was on rollers. That had made the rumbling noise. He took hold of a handle and pushed, but the door wouldn't budge.

"Move, please!" Billy moaned. He pushed again, but the big door barely moved a centimeter no matter how hard his young arms pushed. Finally he gave up.

He walked back toward the pickup. He looked all around. The barn was filled with several stalls lined up in a row. He looked in the first stall. There was a wooden gate about as tall as he was. He pushed a latch and swung the gate open. Old hay covered the floor. A wooden trough was set by the gate. There was a big wooden window where he could see cracks of light. He tried opening the window, but like the heavy wooden door, it wouldn't budge.

Billy left that stall and went to the next. A large black leather horse harness hung on a wooden peg by the gate. Below the harness, an old rusty horseshoe was nailed to the wooden post.

"This is more of a stable than a barn. They must have kept horses in here." As in the stall before, Billy tried the window, but it was either nailed shut or fastened somehow from the outside. Billy didn't waste much time. He quickly walked to the next stall and the next. Each window was shut and would not open. He went inside all eight stalls in the stable. But none of the windows opened. At the far end of the stable was another long wooden door, but it wouldn't roll open either.

Billy remembered the frightened look on his sister's face as the big Asian man tied her arms. He began to feel angry again. He ran back to the pickup.

"There's got to be a way out of here." He thought about breaking one of the windows to get out but decided that would make too much noise. He didn't want to give himself away. He looked in the dim light for any other possible escape route. He saw an old hoe leaning against the wall.

"Maybe I could dig out!" he said softly. He ran and picked up the hoe. He ran to the big rolling door and began to dig. His family had a garden in their backyard at home, so using a hoe wasn't a new experience for the boy. He swung the hoe rapidly into the dirt. The dirt was packed hard and not easy to dig. Billy wondered about giving up, but then thought about his sister and Carlos. He surprised himself at how fast his arms moved.

Chunk by hard chunk, the hole began to grow. A larger hole of light appeared underneath the door. Seeing the light grow encouraged the boy. He dug faster and faster, but then finally had to stop to catch his breath. His chest heaving, he leaned down to stick his head into the hole. He could see to the outside, but barely.

"A shovel would go faster," Billy thought. He dropped the hoe and ran back to the first stall. He looked all around the barn. Then he looked up. A flat wooden ceiling was high above him. Billy stared at the ceiling.

"That could be a loft or an attic. I don't see any rafters like you should on a roof. Maybe there's a way up there, if that's really a loft."

He walked quickly down the row of stalls, looking for a shovel, and at the same time looking up for any possible sign that there was a way into an attic. He got to the last stall without success. Then he saw it, leaning against the far corner at the front of the stable—an old shovel.

Forgetting about the loft, Billy grabbed the shovel and ran back to his hole by the big sliding door. He quickly began digging again. Using the weight of his foot, he found it easier to get a bigger bite out of the dirt floor. Even so, it was rough digging. He wished he had on his heavy work boots instead of his athletic shoes. The rubber soles weren't as good for digging.

Little by little, the hole grew bigger. It seemed like he'd

been digging for an hour to a boy who was in a hurry to go find his friends. After several tests of trying to wiggle through the hole, Billy decided the best way to get out would be to lie on his back and go head first. By this time he was covered with the dark brown dirt. He dug harder and faster, sure he would be able to get out on the next try. When he was satisfied he would be able to slip out of the hole, he dropped the shovel.

He began to wiggle forward and push as best he could with his hands and feet. He wiggled his head through the hole, and then his shoulders. His body was halfway in and halfway out. Once his head was outside, he looked up. He noticed that the roof was peaked and not flat. High above, on the gable near the peak of the roof was a large, square hole, half hidden by a tree branch.

"There must be a loft after all." He groaned, trying to push with his feet. He was so busy squeezing his way out that he didn't notice them at first. Then a dog barked. Billy turned his head. He froze when he saw them. Chan and Mr. Cowboy Hat were coming down the dirt drive that led to the stable. Not only that, Mr. Cowboy Hat held two large black-and-tan Doberman pinschers on a leash.

Seeing Billy, the dogs lunged forward, barking furiously. The two men saw why the dogs were barking. They looked surprised. Chan smiled broadly. He shouted out something. Then they began to run toward Billy.

"Aaccckk!" Billy yelled when he saw them. He tried to wiggle back, but couldn't move. He was stuck! Somehow his shirt was caught on the bottom of the big sliding door. Billy jerked and pulled desperately. He couldn't go forward or backward. The men and the dogs were getting closer by the second. Billy wiggled frantically. The dogs were only ten yards away. They barked furiously, white flecks of saliva flying out of their mouths.

"Looks like we caught a little squirrel in his hole, Chan," Mr. Cowboy Hat said as he walked over. He smiled. Chan nodded. The dogs kept lunging and panting to go forward. "Brutus and Bouser are glad to see you. They like chasing down little squirrels."

"You must be Billy," Chan said. "I guess you hid in the back of the truck. You saved us a trip to the dump. I think you have something that belongs to us."

Billy didn't say a word. Mr. Cowboy Hat was letting the dogs get too close. The boy wiggled once more. There was a rip as his shirtsleeve tore. The boy scooted back through the hole just as the closest Doberman snapped right at his head.

Back inside the stable, everything seemed very dark to the boy. He struggled to his feet. He quickly picked up the old shovel. If he was going to get caught, he planned on giving them a fight. Holding the shovel, he ran for the pickup truck. He opened the driver's side of the door to get inside, but realized that would only trap him. On the floor of the pickup was a cellular phone. He wanted to grab it, but there wasn't time. The big stable door was starting to slide open. Billy slammed the pickup door shut and ran to the far end of the stable, carrying his shovel. He ran into the last stall and hid down by the gate.

"Chan, you stay by the door with Brutus," Mr. Cowboy Hat said loudly over the noise of the barking dogs. "We've got him now."

Billy began to shake as he leaned against the stall gate. Down at the other end of the stable, Mr. Cowboy Hat was holding the leash of the other Doberman. A small stream of sweat ran down Billy's forehead and down his cheek.

"Why don't you come out and save us some trouble, little Billy Squirrel?" Mr. Cowboy Hat called out. "There's no way out of here."

Billy didn't say a word. His chest was pounding so hard he thought for sure that the whole world could hear it.

The man with the cowboy hat was patiently checking each stall, one by one. "Come out, come out wherever you are." His voice was getting closer. Billy was afraid to look. The Doberman whined impatiently. "You don't want me to let Bouser loose, do you, Billy Squirrel?"

The Doberman barked. The gate on the third stall creaked slowly open as the man checked inside. Billy gripped the handle of the shovel tightly. He looked frantically around. He was praying silently when he noticed the ladder. Only it wasn't exactly a ladder. Near the other big sliding door on the other side of the stable were several wooden boards nailed horizontally to the side wall. They led up like a ladder. Billy's eyes followed them up. An indentation in the ceiling looked like it could be an attic door. Billy hadn't noticed it before because the wooden rungs blended so well with the old wooden walls.

"Come on out, Billy Squirrel," Mr. Cowboy Hat said. "I'm getting tired of this little game." The gate of the fourth stall creaked open as the man checked inside. Billy raised his head to peek through a crack in the boards on the stall. Mr. Cowboy Hat came out of the fourth stall and headed for the fifth. He opened the gate. When he began to step inside, Billy made his move.

Gripping the shovel tightly, Billy sprang up and ran for the wooden ladder. He was halfway there when the Doberman began barking furiously. Mr. Cowboy Hat yelled and came out of the stall. Billy dropped the shovel and started up the ladder. Mr. Cowboy Hat cursed as he saw the boy heading up the ladder. He let loose of the leash and the big Doberman rushed forward. Billy grabbed hold of the next rung of wood. He pulled himself up frantically. But as he was reaching for the next rung, the other one suddenly creaked and popped right out of the wall. The nails didn't hold in the rotten wood.

"Whooaaaa!" Billy yelled as he fell back. He landed on his feet, but was totally off balance and kept falling. Bouser was licking his lips, anticipating a chance to get at the boy. He was just a few yards away when Billy hit the ground. The rung of wood in his hand flew loose and hit the Doberman right in the nose. The big dog yelped in pain and stumbled sideways and fell.

Billy jumped to his feet. The big Doberman yelped again, trying to figure out what had interrupted his plans for dinner. Billy didn't wait to apologize. He scrambled back up the ladder.

"Stop!" Mr. Cowboy Hat yelled as he ran. Billy didn't look down. He climbed as quickly as he could over the missing rung and hit the floorboard that covered the ceiling. He was afraid it wouldn't open, like all the windows. But to his relief, the board rose up. Billy shot up through the hole.

The loft was filled with old hay bales. Billy climbed up through the hole as fast as he could move. Then he looked down. Mr. Cowboy Hat was coming right up the ladder after him. The man looked up and smiled at Billy.

"You're making this awful hard, son," the man said with irritated determination. Billy jumped back from the hole. As he did, he tripped on a hay bale. Mr. Cowboy Hat's head poked up through the hole in the loft. He smiled when he saw Billy sprawled out on the floor. But then his smile changed as a loud cracking noise filled the air.

"Noooooooooo!" the man yelled as the board he stood on popped loose. Mr. Cowboy Hat's head suddenly disappeared. Billy heard a thud and loud noises and cursing. "I'll get you, squirt!" the man yelled as he struggled to his feet. As he started back up the ladder, Billy slid the floorboard back over the hole. Then he quickly slid the nearest bale of hay on top of the board.

Even with the hay bale on top of the board, the floorboard began to rise up as Mr. Cowboy Hat began pushing on it. Billy grabbed another hay bale and slid it on top of the board, which slammed down shut under the weight.

"Yeow!" he heard the man yell as the board came down on his head.

Billy could hear the angry man yelling. The boy slid another hay bale on top of the board, and then, with all his strength, he lifted another bale on top of the other three.

"Chan, come help me!" he heard Mr. Cowboy Hat yell. Billy looked frantically around the loft. He tried to lift another hay bale on top of the others, but it was just too high for his young arms. Down below, the dogs were barking, and he could hear voices. Then he felt the vibrations of someone coming up the ladder again. The hay bales began to rise up into the air as the trap door lifted slowly up. Billy took two steps back. The smiling face of Chan appeared as he raised the floorboard with his head. He looked at Billy and began to laugh.

Chapter Eight

A Cornered Squirrel

Billy was amazed that the big Asian man could lift all that hay with just his head. The veins in the man's thick neck bulged as he slowly lifted the floorboard higher.

The whole time he kept looking at Billy and smiling. "You're mine now, little squirrel. Quit making Chan work so hard. We don't have time for foolishness."

Billy didn't wait to reply. He turned and quickly began climbing over the pile of hay that was five or six bales high. While high in the air, on top of the pile of hay, he saw a large square hole of light in the wall of the loft. Billy crawled across the haystack to the light. Behind him, he heard the bales of hay falling as Chan climbed up into the loft.

Billy climbed down the hay bales in front of the large square hole in the gable. The floor was clear by the hole. He jumped down off the last bale of hay. He stuck his head out the square hole in the gable.

Billy looked down sadly. The ground was over twenty feet away, too far to jump. Though he had a big heart for all kinds of adventures, one of the few things he was afraid of was being up too high in the air. He would crawl into dark caves, ride in the back of a garbage truck or even ride his bike down the side of the steepest bluff in town. But if his feet had to leave the ground very far behind, he got nervous.

He looked down at the ground once more. He felt like he was on the high dive at the public swimming pool in Springdale. Most of his friends would go off the high dive with whoops of glee, but not Billy. He had tried several times to go to the end of the diving board. But each time he looked over the edge, he got scared. And the longer he looked down at the water, the farther away it seemed. Once he stood there almost five minutes, peeking over the edge of the board, thinking he would dive but then not diving. The older kids would tease him mercilessly as he walked back to the steps and climbed down. He loved to swim, but the high dive was just too scary.

Then Billy looked up. Above the hole, a five-foot wooden pole stuck out from the gable. At the end of the pole was a large metal pulley. Billy knew there must have been a rope there at one time to help lift the bales of hay up into the loft. But there was no rope that day.

Behind him, he could hear Chan muttering as he climbed over the bales of hay. The big man sounded very angry. Billy looked down once more, hoping somehow that it wouldn't seem so far down. But the ground looked farther away than ever. Billy stared at the wooden pole. He leaned out for a better view. The end of the pole stuck right into a branch of a large oak tree.

"Stay right there!" Chan's voice yelled. The big man had popped his head up over the stack of hay bales. He began lumbering down toward the boy.

Billy felt a tornado of fear raging in his chest and stomach. His friends were in trouble and needed help. He hadn't evaded the mean men this long to give up. But there seemed no place to go except out that hole, and that looked impossible.

"Jesus, help me, please," he said. He took a deep breath. Then he decided he had no choice. He stood on the tiny wooden ledge of the gable hole. Holding onto the edge of the hole with one hand, he reached up toward the wooden pole. His fingertips could touch the wood, but he couldn't quite grab hold. He leaned out of the hole further.

"Stop!" Chan's feet hit the floor. Just as his thick arms reached out, Billy jumped and caught the pole. Before he knew what was happening, he was dangling high in the air over the ground below. His body swung dangerously back and forth from the force of the jump. He held on tightly and then got a better grip. He looked over his shoulder. Chan was reaching out to grab him. Putting hand over hand, Billy moved further away on the pole. Chan watched in disbelief.

"Come back here, you little squirrel!" Chan snarled. But Billy kept going. He didn't look down. He headed toward the tree branch that was touching the pole. It was thinner than he would have liked, but Billy grabbed onto it with one hand. Once he was sure of his grip, he let go of the pole with the other hand. The branch suddenly sagged down under his weight. Billy gasped as he heard the limb moan and creak. But the branch held.

He quickly moved down the branch toward the trunk. Only when he felt like he was safe did he look back at the stable. The big Asian man shook a fist at the boy, then backed out of sight.

Billy moved as fast as he could, but climbing over the smaller branches on the large branch wasn't so easy. He had just reached the trunk of the big oak tree when he heard the dogs barking down below.

"We got you now, treed like a squirrel!" a voice yelled up at the boy. Billy peeked down through the branches. The leaves were so thick that it was hard to see the ground. But far below, he saw both men and the two Dobermans. Billy smiled, feeling a little more confident. He had always envied his friends who climbed trees without much fear. Because of his fear of heights, he had usually stayed out of trees. At that moment, he was higher than he had ever been in any tree. As he caught his breath and settled down, he found the huge tree trunk and branches comforting.

"If I start to fall, I can probably grab a branch, and it'll hold me," Billy whispered. "Lord, help me not to fall. Make me able to hang on tight, just like a squirrel."

"Come down out of there, Billy!" Mr. Cowboy Hat called. "There's no way out. You can't get back into the stable. Quit wasting our time."

"I'm not caught yet," Billy thought. He looked around in the tree, wishing he had a better view. The only way he knew to get a better view was to go higher. He looked up. The large tree seemed to go up forever. "I've got to do it to see where I am." Billy tried to overcome the fear that was so close to taking control of him.

Then he decided. He took a deep breath. Staying near the

trunk of the tree, the ten-year-old boy started climbing. Branch to branch, he carefully climbed up the tree. He tried not to look down, but even when he couldn't help himself, he was so high up and the branches were so thick that he couldn't see the ground. He didn't feel as scared. It meant the two men couldn't see him either. He smiled and climbed higher, imagining himself to be a squirrel.

As he got high into the tree, the top branches began to thin out. For a moment, Billy felt like he was climbing up the mast of an old sailing ship. He climbed past a large bird's nest wedged in one of the upper branches of the tree. He paused to look inside the nest. It was empty except for a few broken pieces of eggshell. Billy wondered what kind of bird had lived in it. "Maybe we can do a study on birds' nests for a home school project. We could all make nests, or better yet, maybe we could find old nests and collect them . . ."

The dogs barking below made Billy forget about the nests. He heard a car engine start. He quickly climbed higher in the tree to see if he could figure out what was happening. Hand over hand, branch after branch, he didn't stop to think or look down. For the moment he forgot about his fear and just concentrated on going higher.

The top of the tree was swaying gently in the late afternoon breeze. Billy clung tightly to the thinning trunk. He'd never imagined he could get so high in a tree. He figured he must be a hundred feet up in the air. The view was spectacular.

From high in the tree the could see a long way in all directions. The huge three-story stone mansion was off to his left. The mansion seemed ancient and creepy. The metal roof had turned green from age. The color reminded Billy of the old statues near the Springdale courthouse. Rusty iron lightning rods stuck up from the roof like giant spears. Iron bars or wooden shutters covered many of the large windows in the mansion. From his angle in the tree, he was looking at the side of the house. Behind the house he could see a big, empty swimming pool with a little bathhouse on one side. Then beyond the pool was a large, fenced flower garden with a high hedge all around it. Tall trees dotted the large lawn. The whole lawn and mansion were surrounded by a stone wall with iron bars on top. There appeared to be only one gate and one driveway into the grounds. The gate was closed. In the center of the gate was a large *W*. Billy saw a stone lion on each side of the gate.

A path from the garden led down to the stable where Billy had been hiding. Riding paths lined with stones led out into the grounds among the trees. Near the stable was a small stone cottage.

Billy looked in the other direction. To the north of the grounds was a large factory. Several big buildings were inside a chainlink fence which surrounded the factory. One building had a tall smokestack reaching high into the sky. The rest of the area outside the stone wall of the mansion grounds seemed deserted. Billy couldn't see any other houses, only trees and open countryside.

Below, a blue sedan headed down the driveway to the gate with the big *W*. The gate swung open by itself as the car got closer. As soon as the car passed through it, the gate closed. The car headed down the tree-lined drive and then turned left, moving north on a small road toward the factory.

"One of them must have left." Billy wasn't sure if that was good or bad. Down below he could hear the Dobermans barking.

"I've got to get out of here and get to a phone." Billy thought about the phone in the pickup truck. All that time he had been alone in the stable, and he could have used the phone to call for help. He groaned at the thought. But with the dogs barking below, in front of the stable, he knew he wouldn't have a chance to get to that phone now. He looked carefully around the grounds.

"I could try to get in the house and find a phone, or I could try to get over the wall somehow and run for help." Looking at the creepy old house made the decision easier. "I'll try to get over the wall. But how?"

Billy looked around the grounds. Heading for the gate would be very risky, he thought, since he would be in the open. And even if he got to the gate, he wasn't sure it would open or if he could squeeze through the bars. Billy frowned and looked around the mansion grounds. Way off behind the garden and little stone cottage was a tree with branches that reached out over the high stone wall.

"If I can get to that tree and climb it, then maybe I can get over the wall and go for help. But how do I get to that tree from here without being seen?"

Perched high in the top of the tall tree, the boy studied the situation carefully. Then he smiled. He had a great idea.

"They called me a squirrel, and that's just what I'll be." Billy began climbing down. With each step, he looked carefully down through the leaves and branches, hoping he wouldn't see the dogs or whoever else might be waiting below. If he could see them, then they might see what he was trying to do. After climbing a few minutes, he reached the branch he was looking for. He looked down below once more. The branch stretched over the roof of the stable.

Billy began to crawl on the long, heavy branch. At first it was easy, but as the branch got thinner, he had to slow down. He was also scared of being discovered. When the boy was about ten feet away from the roof of the stable, he stopped. Billy saw Mr. Cowboy Hat over by the base of the tree, sitting on a metal folding chair underneath the tree. The man held a long hunting knife in one hand and a stick of wood in the other. He slowly peeled slivers of wood off the stick. The big blade glinted in the sunlight. He worked the wood patiently, occasionally looking up the trunk of the tree. Luckily, his back was toward the stable.

The two big Dobermans were pacing around the bottom of the tree. They looked up. Once in a while, one of the dogs would jump up and put his front legs on the trunk of the tree as if he wanted to climb it.

Billy moved on down the branch slowly. He knew that he could be discovered at any moment if the man turned around. He didn't know if Dobermans had good eyesight or not. Some dogs had excellent sight, but a lot of dogs mostly used their sense of smell or hearing.

"Those dogs seem to use their teeth and mouths more to me," Billy thought as he inched along the branch. He tried not to look straight down.

"I'm a squirrel. I'm a squirrel," he said to himself as he moved along the branch. A few times, he closed his eyes so he wouldn't see the ground below.

After a few more minutes, he was on the part of the branch that hung over the roof. Billy didn't want to drop down just yet since he figured not enough branch would be hiding him. He kept inching along, and was pleasantly surprised as the branch began to sag slowly down to the roof under his weight.

"Just like an elevator," Billy thought as he lifted his leg over the branch. His foot hit the wooden shake shingles of the stable silently. Billy lifted the other leg over as quietly as possible. He crouched down and let go of the branch.

The branch snapped out of his hands and shot back up. The leaves shook as the small branches trembled. Billy quickly scrambled around to the other side of the leaves as he heard the dogs begin to bark. He froze. The dogs barked louder and louder. Billy wasn't sure whether to climb back into the tree or climb up over the peak of the roof or to just sit still. He sat still, frozen, praying that no one would find him.

The dogs continued to bark loudly. Then they seemed to settle down. Billy peeked carefully through the branches. The blue sedan he had seen leave earlier now pulled to a stop in front of the stable. Chan got out of the driver's side. He walked over to Mr. Cowboy Hat.

"I have brought the children from the warehouse," Chan said. "I take them inside with others. We will see if Mr. Jeremy is trying to double-cross Mr. Wu."

"It's worth a try," Mr. Cowboy Hat drawled. "I never seen such a mixed-up deal in my life. I can't imagine even a fool like Jeremy would try to use a bunch of kids to help him."

"Something not right." Chan shook his head. "Mr. Wu say to get to the bottom of this before we can get truck."

"We ain't going to get that truck until we get that squirrelly kid out of this tree. Tom Worthington won't talk no matter what. I think we could threaten to kill him, and he still wouldn't talk."

"Killing come later, after we get truck." Chan wasn't smiling.

"But what about these kids?"

"Mr. Wu have good idea. But first we need to see what they know and if they work for Jeremy. Then we can use them to get Squirrel Boy out of tree." Chan walked over to the sedan. He opened the door. Three children wearing blindfolds slid out of the back seat, their hands tied behind their backs. Then Chan took off the blindfolds. Billy's mouth dropped open when he realized the three children were Josh, Emily and Julie.

"We go up to house," Chan said sternly to the children. Billy could hear every word. "No funny business." The man pointed to a stone-lined path that led up toward the house. Josh and the others began walking without saying a word.

"You stay by tree until squirrel come down," Chan instructed. Mr. Cowboy Hat nodded and resumed peeling off shavings of wood with the big hunting knife. Soon Chan and the three children were out of sight.

"What are they doing here?" Billy almost said out loud. He quickly crawled up the slope of the roof to the peak so he could see over the edge. He was almost totally exposed, but Billy didn't care. He had to see what was happening to his friends.

Mr. Chan led the three children along a path beside the hedged garden, beyond the swimming pool to a patio at the rear of the house. He opened a heavy wooden door. Josh, Emily and Julie walked into the house. Chan followed them inside. The big heavy door slammed shut. Billy leaned over the edge of the roof, wondering what he should do.

Chapter Nine

Mr. Wu

Move faster," the big Asian man ordered as Josh, Emily and Julie walked through a large kitchen in the old mansion.

"You're going to be sorry you kidnapped us," Josh said, trying to sound brave. His voice cracked, and he was afraid that Chan didn't believe one word.

"Ha, ha. Chan already sorry he ever see you kids," the big man replied. "You all cause trouble. But we get to the bottom of this."

The children walked out of the kitchen and down a long hall which led into a big room with a large table. The table was covered with a plain white linen tablecloth. An empty golden vase sat in the center.

"Some dining room," Julie whispered.

"You could feed an army in here," Emily replied.

"Keep going," Chan instructed. They walked out the other

end of the dining room and came into a large living room filled with luxurious antique couches, chairs, tables and lamps. A huge crystal chandelier hung from the high ceiling. Large paintings covered the walls. All were portraits of serious-looking men and women. The men had long beards and mustaches, and the women wore fancy high-necked dresses. Their faces stared out into the room like silent guardians from the past.

"I feel like I'm being watched," Julie said, looking up at the paintings.

"Me too," Josh said glumly.

"Up the stairs." Chan pointed to a large winding staircase at the far end of the room.

The children started up the steps. Another huge chandelier hung in the center of the winding circular staircase. There were dozens of steps. When they got to the top, Josh stopped.

"Next floor," Chan said tersely. Josh nodded and began climbing again. All the steps were beginning to make him breathe harder. Finally, they reached the next landing.

"Down hall, first door on right," the big Asian man said. The children stopped at the door. He took a long key from his pocket and opened the door.

"You know these children?" Chan asked as he opened the door.

"Carlos!" Julie yelled when she saw her brother. He was sitting on a plain wooden chair. The small room was long and narrow, as if it was some kind of closet. A small window was covered with bars.

"Rebecca!" Julie exclaimed.

"You children are friends then?" Chan demanded.

"Yes, we're friends," Josh said. He thought he would see Billy.

"How long have you worked for Jeremy Worthington?" Chan inquired.

"We've never worked for him," Josh said. "I told you that before."

The big man was silent. Then his eyes seemed to light up. He smiled.

"Then you must work for Tom Worthington?" Chan questioned.

"I'm telling you, we've never heard of Tom Worthington or Jeremy Worthington," Josh said. "And we don't work for either one of them."

"Wait a minute," Emily said. "I've heard those names before, I think. They have something to do with the Worthington factory."

"Aha!" Chan said. "You do know them."

"No, I just read about them in a computer magazine or newspaper," Emily said. "They were in an article about the release of the new Z-5000 microprocessor. That's where I heard those names before."

"Hmmmm. We'll see. You children wait here together. I return." Chan walked out, closing the door. They all heard the lock click, then footsteps going down the hall. As soon as he left, Josh tried the doorknob.

"Forget it," Carlos said. "I already tried."

"How did you guys get here?" Emily asked Rebecca and Carlos.

"What about you?" Rebecca asked the others with just as much amazement.

"You wouldn't believe it," Emily said.

"Well, I know you won't believe what happened to us either," Rebecca replied. "It all started when Billy tried to get a hamster cage out of the dumpster behind the toystore."

Rebecca and Carlos quickly began telling them the story of how they had gotten trapped in the dumpster and hauled away by the garbage truck to the landfill. Josh and the others listened with their mouths open.

"You actually got dumped out of a garbage truck?" Julie asked Carlos. "Are you okay?"

"We were doing fine," Carlos said.

"Yeah, until that Chan and Mr. Cowboy Hat came to the dump and brought us back here," Rebecca said. "It has something to do with those boxes of computer chips."

"You're right about that," Emily said. "Listen to what happened to us."

She quickly began telling them about finding the computer chips in the alley and all the events that led up to their capture. Carlos shook his head in surprise.

"So now Chan thinks we may be working with the guy with the red beard, stealing computer chips or something."

"Red Beard must be Jeremy or Tom Worthington," Josh said slowly. "But what happened to Billy?"

"The last I saw him he was at the dump," Carlos said. "But like I told you, he got a plastic bag with a piece of paper and a key out of one of those boxes of computer chips. That's what Chan and Red Beard must be looking for, not just the chips."

"But why didn't they catch him at the dump?" Emily asked.

"Because he went to look at the bulldozer right before they showed up in that pickup truck," Rebecca replied. "He must have seen us get tied up. At least I hope he did."

"Maybe he ran away and called for help," Emily offered.

"That's possible," Josh said seriously. "But how would he

know where we are? *I'm* not sure where we are."

"This has to be the Worthington estate," Emily said. "I've heard about this house before. There's no other old house like this anywhere close to Springdale."

"You're probably right," Josh said.

"But none of this makes sense," Emily said. "Why would the Worthingtons steal chips from their own factory?"

"I don't know," Josh said. "Who is Chan and the guy in the cowboy hat? And who is this Mr. Wu they keep talking about?"

The children heard footsteps in the hall. They backed away from the door. The doorknob turned. The door opened. Chan pushed the man with the red beard into the room. Red Beard looked extremely nervous as he stared at the children.

"You know this man?" Chan demanded. He looked at each child's face.

"We never saw him before today," Julie said.

"I never saw him until just now," Rebecca added. "Who are you?"

"That's none of your business," the man with the red beard said nervously. "I told you they didn't know me. You've got to explain to Mr. Wu that I'm keeping up my end of the deal, just like we promised."

"Tell him yourself." Chan pointed toward the door. A small, old Asian man with wire-rim glasses walked into the room. He looked silently at the children and then at the man with the red beard.

"Mr. Wu," Red Beard almost pleaded, "you've got to believe me. I never saw these children before today. I swear. I don't know how they found out about the chips. I brought those three from Springdale because that girl had found the chips where we tried to—"

"I've heard your story," Mr. Wu interrupted. He spoke quietly, and almost sounded polite. But his unfeeling eyes were still full of questions. "Perhaps your cousin knows these children."

Red Beard looked puzzled and then hopeful. He rubbed his sweaty palms on the sides of his pants.

"Yeah, maybe Tom knows them," Red Beard said enthusiastically. "He was in the alley too. He's the one who tried to double-cross you, not me. He tried to run, remember?"

The old Asian man's face remained like stone. His thin lips were pressed tightly together. He stared at the children for a moment. He looked at Chan and barked out an order in a foreign language. Chan quickly left the room.

"We shall see what your cousin says," Mr. Wu said.

"Did he regain consciousness?" Red Beard asked.

"He will talk to me."

"I bet he's the one. I've had a feeling all along that he had other partners."

"We thought his partners would be the FBI, not children," Mr. Wu.

"He wouldn't go to the FBI. He wanted the money for himself. He's a worse thief than I ever was."

Mr. Wu looked silently at the nervous man. Then he looked down at his watch. He frowned. "Time is running short."

Footsteps could be heard in the hall, coming closer. A few seconds later Chan appeared, holding another man by the shoulder. The man's face was pale except for big purplish bruises on his cheeks. His forehead was covered in sweat. His short blond hair was tousled. His eyes were watery. He looked as if he would have fallen down if the big Asian man hadn't hadn't been holding him up.

"Chair!" Chan demanded. Rebecca hopped off the wooden chair that he wanted. Chan then forced the young man to sit in the chair. He rolled his head sideways and looked at the children blankly.

"You know these children, Tom?" Mr. Wu asked.

"No . . . no, sir, I don't, Mr. Wu." Tom wheezed and then coughed.

"Are you sure?"

"Yes, I'm sure," the young man said. "Please don't hurt me anymore. I told you everything I know."

"Everything but who is working with you." Mr. Wu turned to the row of children. "You know this man?"

"No," said Josh.

"Me neither," Emily added. The other children shook their heads except Carlos.

Mr. Wu stared at Carlos.

"I don't know him," Carlos said. "But I remember seeing him in the alley. He's the guy who was driving the limousine."

"Oh, yeah, that's right," Rebecca replied. Then she got scared as she looked at Mr. Wu. "But we don't know him. We never saw him before today."

"There was no one else in the alley," Red Beard protested. "I was right there."

"We were there," Carlos said. "We got trapped in the dumpster."

"Where?" Mr. Wu asked.

"We were in the dumpster behind the toystore," Carlos said. Then he and Rebecca began to explain to the old man what happened. Chan began to smile as the children told their story. Red Beard began to look a little less nervous. Mr. Wu only looked surprised.

"Mr. Chan and that guy with the cowboy hat found us at the dump," Rebecca said. "But we didn't help anybody and don't know anything. In fact, I still don't know what's going on. My brother Billy has the plastic bag you're looking for. At least he did have it, the last time we saw him. Only he didn't know what it was, I'm sure. I just want to go home."

"That's right," Josh insisted. "I told you that we were just looking for them when Emily found the computer chips in the alley. They must have fallen out of the box or something. We didn't do anything, and we want to go home now. Please let us go home."

The man with blond hair and bruises stared at the children. He groaned as he shifted in his seat. Mr. Wu held a finger up to his thin lips, thinking. He looked at the children once more. "The boy, Billy, is your brother?" Mr. Wu asked Rebecca.

"Yes," Rebecca said. "The last time I saw him, he was at the dump."

Chan smiled. He spoke rapidly to Mr. Wu in a foreign language. Mr. Wu listened carefully. A slight expression of surprise crossed the old man's face. He spoke in the foreign language to Chan.

"Your brother in tree," Chan grunted.

"What?" Rebecca asked.

"Your brother is hiding in a tree by the stable outside," Mr. Wu said carefully.

"What?" Rebecca asked in surprise. "Billy in a tree? That's crazy. He's scared of heights."

"Brother like squirrel," Chan said with anger and disgust.

"If he has the key and map, then let's just go get him," Red Beard insisted. "We can get back on schedule. The plan will still work out."

"What about the children?" Mr. Wu asked Red Beard.

"Let's talk outside." Red Beard glanced at the children briefly and then looked away. The old man nodded. Chan held open the door. Mr. Wu walked out first and then Red Beard. The door shut and the lock clicked. No one said anything until their footsteps sounded far away.

Josh listened at the door. Then he turned to face the others. Julie stooped over the man sitting in the chair. She tenderly wiped his forehead with her shirttail. The man looked up at her with grateful eyes.

"What are we going to do?" Rebecca asked fearfully.

"I don't know." Josh looked at the man in the chair with concern. "We need to get out of here. All of us need to get out of here. We need to get Billy and run far away."

The man with the blond hair tried to stand. He wobbled to his feet, but then his legs gave out. He fell back down into the chair and moaned.

"Don't try to move," Julie said softly. "You're too hurt."

"She's right," Josh said. "What's your name?"

"I'm Tom Worthington," the man gasped out. "This is my parents' house. I am not a thief! You've got to believe me."

"What?" Josh asked.

"I was only trying to help," the man said breathlessly. "I was only trying to . . ."

The man stopped speaking. His head slumped over to one side awkwardly. His eyes were closed and his face seemed as pale as a sheet of paper. Rebecca put her hand over her mouth. She would have screamed, but no sound came out of her mouth. All the other children stepped back, staring at the man hunched over in the chair.

"Is he dead?" Carlos asked. No one said a word.

Chapter Ten

On the Run

Billy sat on top of the roof of the stable, hidden in the branches of the big oak tree. He stared at the big heavy door of the old mansion for the longest time, unsure of what to do. He'd been praying the whole time, but didn't feel like he was getting any clear answers. Then Chan and another small Asian man finally came out of the door and walked toward the stable. The two men talked in a foreign language. Not even one syllable made sense to the boy.

"I wish I could interpret tongues," Billy thought to himself. The two men walked over to Mr. Cowboy Hat.

"Of course he's still up there," Mr. Cowboy Hat said. "I've been sitting here the whole time."

"Billy, come down!" Chan shouted up into the tree. One of the Dobermans barked. "Come down and we'll take you to your friends."

"He's scared of heights, according to his sister," Mr. Wu

said to the man with the cowboy hat. "He must be sitting up there, scared to come down. I want you to climb up and get him and the bag. We don't have time to wait."

"Yes, sir," Mr. Cowboy Hat said, though not with enthusiasm. "I'll get him down or throw him down."

"Whichever is the fastest," the small Asian man replied.

Billy watched with surprise at how quickly Mr. Cowboy Hat started climbing the tree. The big man made it look like he was merely climbing a ladder.

"I've got to get out of here," Billy thought. "I'll go over the wall and call for help, just like I planned."

Being careful to be as quiet as possible, Billy began creeping up over the peak of the stable roof and started down the other side. He hated leaving the covering of the tree branch, but there was no other way. He crawled carefully down the roof, cringing each time one of the old wooden shingles creaked. He could see the mansion clearly, and anyone on that side of the stable would be able to see him if they looked up. Luckily, he could hear Chan and Mr. Cowboy Hat yelling on the other side of the stable. As long as they thought he was in the tree, he was safe.

Crawling down the steep roof was scary. But Billy had a destination. Another tree branch touched the edge of the stable roof. Billy crawled straight to it. Soon he was touching its leaves. He wasn't sure what kind of tree it was, but he knew by the leaves that it wasn't an oak. The tree was much smaller, and the branch didn't look nearly as strong as he had hoped. Billy grabbed hold of the thickest part of the branch and tried to crawl out into the tree. He tried not to look down, but it was impossible.

He got a good grip on the branch and stepped off the roof

with one leg. The branch bent down. Billy then reached out further and stepped off the roof with his other leg. The branch sagged suddenly under his weight. The downward motion caused him to lose his balance and he rolled to one side, from the top of the branch all the way around to the bottom. The leaves rattled and shook as the branch swayed in the air under the boy's weight.

Billy held on as tight as he could. He was hanging underneath the branch with his back facing the ground. His hands and feet were clamped tightly onto the branch. He imagined he looked like a sloth at the zoo, hanging upside down. The swaying branch finally stopped moving.

Once again, Billy decided that looking down would be a bad idea. He tried to move as fast as he could down the branch toward the tree trunk. He would reach out with his feet as far as he could go and then slide the rest of his body along. His arms and legs soon felt very heavy. Just as he got to the trunk, his feet slipped and his legs fell. His arms felt like they would be jerked out of their sockets, but Billy held on tight.

"Whoa!" Billy said automatically. His body rocked back and forth, his arms aching. Billy tried to reach the tree trunk with his feet, but it was still too far. Knowing that his arms wouldn't last too much longer, he began heading hand over hand toward the trunk. When he was almost sure he would have to let go, his foot finally found a resting place on a lower branch. Billy pulled himself over to the tree trunk and sat down, hugging the trunk.

For several moments all he could do was shake. But then he heard voices. He quickly began climbing down the smaller tree. The ground got closer and closer. Billy jumped the last three feet.

He felt like kissing the safe ground, but he didn't have time. He had to keep moving. Everything looked different on the ground from how it had up high in the tree. The tree that he planned to use to escape over the wall looked far away. There was a lot of open space in between where he could be easily seen if someone passed by.

"I've got to try it." He began to walk and then decided to run. He hadn't gone ten steps when he heard the dog bark. He stopped and looked around. Near the corner of the stable one of the Doberman pinschers was looking right at him. The dog looked puzzled, but not for long. It barked again and jolted in Billy's direction.

"Yikes!" Billy screamed. Heading toward the stone wall was out of the question. Billy ran for the hedge of the big garden. He tore around the hedge like he was running a race. He could tell from the sound of the dog's furious barking that the dog was gaining fast. Billy rounded the corner of the hedge, his feet flying. Then he saw the tall iron gate right in front of him. He slipped in the grass trying to stop. The barking dog was just around the corner. Billy half crawled and leaped to the gate. He pushed down on the latch and the gate popped open. He scrambled inside. He shut the gate just as Bouser lunged toward him. The big dog's nose pressed through the bars on the gate, barking furiously. Billy scooted back away from the dog.

"He's on the run!" he heard someone yell. Billy didn't wait to see who was coming. He ran past the beds of flowers and shrubs deep into the garden. The garden path twisted and turned. In the center of the garden was a fountain. A little statue of a man held a pitcher that poured a continuous stream of water into a pool covered with lily pads and little stone islands. Billy kept running. Far behind him he could hear the dog barking loudly.

"As soon they get to the gate, they'll let that dog in," Billy thought. He tore past a bed of beautiful red and orange roses in front of a small wooden gazebo. He thought about climbing up on the gazebo, but there was no good place to start climbing. So he ran on. Beyond the gazebo was a small orchard of apple trees. Beyond them Billy could see the distant hedge.

Though he was panting hard, Billy ran through the little grove of apple trees and headed for the hedge. He ran along the hedge looking for a possible gate or hole big enough to climb out. But the hedge was thick and tight. Hardly a bird could get through it. Billy ran from one end to the other frantically looking for a way out. In the distance the dog was still barking furiously. Besides the barking he could hear voices. They would catch up to him soon.

Billy ran back down the length of the hedge, nearly panicking as he searched for a way out. Then he saw it, just beyond the corner of the hedge near a wheelbarrow. Behind the wheelbarrow he saw what looked like a hole under the hedge. He ran for it.

He slid down on his belly and aimed for the hole. The thick hedge stuck to his clothes and scratched his arms, but Billy didn't care. He scooted and wiggled and before he knew it, his head popped out the other side. He pulled the rest of his body through. Behind him, the barking of the dog grew louder. Billy looked at the distant stone wall and knew he wouldn't make it. That left only one other option—the mansion. Maybe he could find a phone inside and call 911 before anyone found him. He tore across the lawn, past the little stone cottage, then past the back of the swimming pool bathhouse. He paused, waiting by the bathhouse.

The big wooden door of the mansion was nearby, but to get to it, he'd have to be completely in the open. Billy decided he had no choice. He ran for the big door. He reached it in a few seconds. He turned the knob, but the door wouldn't open. He tried again, but it was definitely locked.

Billy looked toward the stable and garden. No one was in sight, but he could still hear the dog barking and voices shouting inside the garden.

"That dog will find the hole I went out of soon enough," Billy thought. "There must be another way inside."

Billy ran away from the door around to the other side of the mansion. The building seemed especially huge and long to run around since he was trying to find a door. He didn't stop until he rounded a corner and found himself at the front of the mansion. He ran up the stone steps and tried the front door. Again it was locked.

"He's by the mansion!" a voice shouted. Billy looked off to his left. Coming up the driveway from the direction of the stable was Mr. Cowboy Hat holding the other Doberman on a leash. The dog saw Billy and began howling. Mr. Cowboy Hat smiled and let go of the leash. The Doberman shot out in a dead run.

Billy turned and ran back the way he'd come. The closest tree would be too far away. He knew that if he went too far, he would probably meet the other Doberman coming out of the garden. Billy rounded the corner of the house, looking desperately for something to climb on. That's when he spied the old metal drainpipe running down the corner of the house.

He started climbing. Hand over hand, up he went. His feet

found just enough bite in the cracks of the stones to help him climb. Higher and higher he went till he reached a ledge on the second floor. He tried a window at the ledge but it wouldn't open. Then he flattened down as he heard the sound of barking.

Mr. Cowboy Hat's Doberman rounded the corner of the house and just kept going. Billy waited until the dog had gone around the next corner before standing up. He tried the window once more, but it wouldn't budge. He was afraid to look down.

Up above, he saw a little stone balcony jutting out of the side of the mansion. He began climbing up the drainpipe again. A few moments later he pulled himself up over the stone rail of the balcony. A small door led into the house, but it was locked. The ledge leading around the house on the third floor was wider than the ledge on the second floor.

Billy climbed out of the balcony and onto the ledge. He looked down for an instant and regretted it. The ground looked very far away. He froze. He felt like he was looking down from the high dive, only this was worse since there was no ladder to climb down. His feet refused to move for a long moment.

"I've got to keep going. Help me, God." Billy looked away from the ground and inched along the ledge. He came to a window with bars on it. He gripped the bars thankfully to rest. He looked down once more to see if anyone was coming. He was surprised to hear voices yelling.

Billy looked around fearfully. He expected to see Mr. Cowboy Hat or Chan come into view. But these voices came from the wrong direction. He turned around and looked inside the window. Josh and Carlos were right beyond the glass.

"In here, in here!" they yelled.

"I can't get in!" Billy said, trying not to shout. He was so happy to see his friends that not shouting was hard. He pointed to the bars. Josh nodded his head that he understood. Rebecca and the others rushed over to the window.

Just then, the door inside the room began to open, and Billy ducked out of sight. He didn't know who was coming in, but he didn't want to be discovered. He scooted down the ledge to the next window. It was also covered with bars. Billy kept moving. He rounded the corner of the house and found another balcony. He was at the front of the mansion now. He carefully climbed up over the small stone rail and ducked down. He peeked through the rails. In the distance he could see Mr. Cowboy Hat looking all around, up in trees and around bushes. The big dog was still barking, running frantically, sniffing the ground.

A door was behind Billy. He reached up his hand, praying silently. He took hold of the knob and turned. Nothing happened. Then he turned the knob the other direction. This time it moved. He heard a click and the door swung open into the room. Billy crawled in and slowly shut the door.

Billy found himself in a large dim room. The curtains on the windows and doors blocked out most of the light. He paused to let his eyes adjust. He crawled across the floor to a large bed. He raised his head and peeked around. The room seemed empty. Outside he could hear voices in the hallway. Footsteps moved down the hall and came toward the door. Billy ducked behind the bed and waited.

He expected the door to burst open and someone to flash on a light. But the steps kept moving and voices grew fainter. Billy raised his head. He saw what he wanted on the other side of the bed. On an antique wooden table was a lovely, old black dial telephone.

Billy scooted around the bed quickly. He picked up the phone, and for the first time in a long time, he gave a sigh of relief. "At last," he thought. He dialed *911* and lifted the phone to his ear. He waited, trying to think what he would say to the police. But the phone didn't ring. Billy tried the number again.

"Come on." He clicked down the receiver several times. He couldn't hear a dial tone. He dialed again, but it was no use. The phone was dead.

Chapter Eleven

The Chase

Billy stared at the old phone in disbelief and disgust. His heart began pounding hard again as he realized he had to make more decisions. "Maybe the phone is just too old to work." He followed the wire leading away from the phone to the place where it disappeared into the wall. Everything looked in order.

Crawling across the floor, Billy saw a hole of light at the door. He crawled closer. The light was coming through the keyhole. The boy put his eye up to the hole and peered out. He saw a long hall with several doors. He looked down two doors on his right. That should be the room where he had seen his sister and friends. He stared carefully down the hall. He looked at the door. He smiled when he saw a long key sticking out of the lock. He waited for another moment, but didn't hear or see anyone.

"I've got to try at least." Billy stood up and turned the

doorknob as slowly as he could so it wouldn't make a sound. The door opened. Billy suddenly stopped pulling as the door began to creak. No matter how slowly he pulled it, it still creaked. Holding his breath, he kept pulling until he could slip out the door.

Once in the hall, he tiptoed softly past the doors. He stopped in front of the second door on his right. He could hear Josh's voice and Rebecca's. He didn't knock or say a word. He reached down and slowly turned the key. The lock clicked. He turned the knob and pushed open the door.

"Billy!" Rebecca yelled.

"Shhhhhhhhsssshhhh!" Billy said. He stepped inside and quickly closed the door. His sister ran and hugged him as his other friends gathered all around, slapping his back and patting his arm.

"How did you get here?" Emily asked with amazement.

"It's too long a story," Billy replied seriously. "The problem is how we are going to get out. They're outside looking for me. They've got two big dogs. I tried using a phone in the other room, but it didn't work."

"All the phones are dead," a man said. For the first time, Billy noticed the man with bruised cheeks sitting in the chair. His face looked tired and haggard, but something looked familiar about him.

"I've seen you before," Billy said slowly. Then he remembered. "You were the guy in the alley today driving the limousine."

Billy stepped back, suddenly afraid.

Josh smiled when he saw his friend's reaction. He patted Billy on the back. "It's all right. He's one of the good guys. He's Tom Worthington, and this is his parents' house. He was helping stop a robbery of his family's business, but things backfired. He was working with the Round Rock police and the FBI. If we only could get out of here and phone them and let them know where we are and what happened."

"All the phones in the house are cut off," Tom Worthington repeated. "I heard them talking. They were afraid of something going wrong or of possible wiretaps. They're using cellular phones."

"Cellular phones!" Billy said excitedly. "I saw a cellular phone in the pickup truck that's parked out in the stable. We could use that phone."

Then the boy's face fell. Chan and the other men plus the dogs were all outside looking frantically for him.

"The stable?" Tom Worthington's pale face seemed brighter.

"Yeah," Billy said. "I was hiding in there earlier. I hid in the back of the pickup truck when it left the dump."

"So that's how you got here," Rebecca said. "Then they said you were hiding in a tree. None of us believed them because you don't like climbing trees."

"I was in the tree, but it wasn't because I wanted to be up there," Billy replied. "But now we're stuck here. They'll catch us for sure if we go outside."

"No, there's a way," Tom Worthington said slowly. "We can get to the stable."

"But the dogs and other men are outside," Billy said. "They're bound to see us. We couldn't get near there."

"There's another way." The man touched his swollen cheek with his hand. "We just have to get down to the basement."

"What are waiting for then?" Billy asked. He opened the

door with a smile. Rebecca paused, looking fearfully in the hall.

"What if they come back?" she asked.

"We'll just have to risk it," Tom Worthington said. "If we don't move quickly, Mr. Wu and Jeremy and the others will all get away. We've got to hurry."

Tom Worthington limped painfully out of the room and into the hall. Billy was right behind them, followed by the others. Tom hobbled down the hall to the large staircase. He held onto the old wooden banister and started down the steps. He cringed in pain with each step.

"Let me help you," Billy said, reaching out to Tom. The young man smiled and held onto Billy's hand. Side by side they went down the long steps, past the second floor to the first floor.

"To the kitchen." Without pausing Tom led the way through the living room, into the dining room and into the kitchen. He suddenly stopped. Outside, coming up the steps was Chan. The big Asian man saw Tom and the children and began running toward the kitchen.

"To the basement!" Tom yelled. He ran as best he could across the kitchen to a door beside the pantry. He opened the door and motioned for the children to go down the steps. The girls went first, then Josh and Carlos. Billy was standing by Tom when the kitchen door opened. Chan bolted inside. He snarled when he saw Billy.

The other children were almost stumbling down the steps. Chan rushed across the room. Billy ducked through the door, and Tom followed close behind, slamming the door shut. He quickly turned the key that he knew would be in the door.

"Keep going! Keep going!" Tom shouted.

The children waited at the bottom of the steps for Billy and Tom. The young man looked back up the stairs. Chan was pounding on the door, twisting the knob.

"That will hold him awhile. Follow me." Tom led them across the dark, damp basement, past a huge iron furnace and an old water heater. Beyond that was an old coal chute by a window. Boxes and trunks and old furniture were scattered about. On the far wall was an old set of wooden shelves. Tools and old paint cans sat on the shelves. Tom headed straight for them.

"Help me move this." Tom reached up and began sliding the shelves out sideways. Josh helped him push too. Paint cans and tools fell to the floor. Billy gasped when he saw a door appear behind the shelves. Tom pushed the door open. A dark hole appeared.

"A tunnel!" Billy said in surprise.

"It goes to the stable," Tom said. "My grandfather had it built years ago so he could slip in or out of the house unnoticed."

Tom flipped a light switch on the wall inside the tunnel, but no lights came on. "The lights must be out. No one has used this in years. Never mind. Let's go. Josh, you wait with me."

Billy and Carlos headed into the musty darkness, followed by the three girls. Once they were inside, they waited.

"Help me pull the shelf back over the door," Tom said. Josh nodded. Standing in the secret doorway, they both grabbed the heavy wooden shelf and rocked it back and forth until it was in place. When they were almost done, they heard a gunshot. Then they heard footsteps coming down the basement stairs.

"Let's go," Tom whispered. He closed the door behind them and everyone was covered in total darkness. Tom walked in the darkness past the others. "Everyone hold hands and follow me."

The young man limped along in complete darkness. The others followed without saying a word. The tunnel was damp and almost cold. When Billy brushed against the wall, it felt moist on his arm.

They seemed to be walking forever when a glimmer of light appeared ahead of them. Tom stopped when the light was right above them. He let go of Julie's hand and began climbing a wooden ladder. He lifted up a wooden floorboard and light spilled down into the tunnel. The children blinked and squinted because the light was so bright.

Tom climbed up the ladder slowly until he was all the way out. The trap door was right next to the first stall, just a few feet away from the parked pickup truck. Tom crawled across the floor and opened the door of the old truck. Just like Billy had said, the phone was lying on the floorboard of the old truck.

"What's he doing?" Josh asked. Billy climbed up the ladder to peek. He could see Tom talking on the phone. Tom was smiling.

"He's talking to someone," Billy whispered excitedly.

"He's got someone," Josh repeated to the others down in the tunnel.

Tom began crawling back across the stable floor to the trap door. He was just starting to climb down when Julie saw a light, only this light was coming from the other end of the tunnel.

"Someone's coming!" Julie warned.

"Up the ladder!" Tom urged. No one had to be told twice. Tom scrambled across the floor to the cab of the pickup. He flung open the passenger door, then turned the key. The engine turned over slowly. The three girls piled into the cab, followed by Carlos.

"We can ride in the back!" Billy pulled himself into the back of the truck, followed by Josh.

"Let's go!" Josh pounded on the roof of the cab. He and Billy crouched down. The engine groaned and grumbled as if it had bad indigestion.

"Come on!" Billy moaned. Out of the corner of his eye he saw Chan's thick head pop up out of the hole. The big man looked furious. The engine roared to life. Tom jammed the truck into reverse gear and shot out of the stable backward.

Jeremy Worthington, Mr. Wu and Mr. Cowboy Hat were walking around the corner when they saw the old pickup truck roar out into the dusty driveway. They looked totally surprised to see Tom Worthington behind the wheel with the children sitting next to him.

Chan came running out of the stable and headed straight for the truck. The big man was pulling a gun out of the waistband of his pants as he got closer. The back tires spun up a cloud of dust as the truck lurched forward. Chan was having trouble getting the gun out of his fat waistline.

Chan ran for the blue sedan parked near the big oak tree. The other men jumped into the car as Chan started it. Tom approached the closed gate and sped up.

"Hold on!" he yelled. He pressed down harder on the accelerator. The truck hit the gate with a horrible crashing sound. The big iron gate popped open as if it were exploding. The pickup truck didn't even slow down. Tom held the wheel steady as he guided the truck down the tree-lined driveway. He looked into the side-view mirror and floored the accelerator.

The blue sedan was fishtailing as it came through the gate. The rear of the car swerved and crashed into one of the stone buttresses. The car slid sideways out of the gate and side-swiped a tree. The sedan kept going in the grass along the road.

Billy cheered when he saw the sedan leave the driveway. The blue car was going much slower and the pickup was pulling away. But Chan got the car back on the driveway, and it too picked up speed.

Tom turned the corner onto the highway going as fast as he could. He sped down the road toward the factory. The blue sedan's tires screeched as it came onto the road behind them.

"Uh oh," Billy said as the blue car began gaining on them. "He's getting closer."

"I know," Josh said glumly.

The pickup started up a small hill. The sedan moved closer. Chan was reaching out the window with his left hand and driving with his right.

"He's got a gun!" Billy yelled.

The pickup sped over the hill and out of sight of the car. Suddenly the truck slowed down and pulled off the road.

"What's he doing?" Billy yelled. The blue sedan shot up over the hill so fast that its front tires left the ground. But then it began swerving and sliding as it tried to stop. It slid sideways off the highway and into the ditch, groaning to a halt.

Billy turned around. Right in front of him, four police cars with lights flashing were passing the pickup truck and heading for the blue sedan stalled in the ditch. Josh smiled and patted his friend on the back as the pickup slowly rolled to a stop.

"Looks like the cavalry finally showed up," Josh said.

"Yeah, finally," Billy said, taking in a deep breath. He looked back at the sedan. The police had the car surrounded. Chan and the other men were struggling out of the car, their hands up in the air. The police were waiting with handcuffs.

Josh climbed slowly out of the truck. He reached up his hand to help Billy down.

"I guess we're going to miss music practice tonight," Billy said, looking down at his watch.

"I think you're right," Josh said with a smile.

Chapter Twelve

The Good Side

All the Home School Detectives were having a great time at the Round Rock police station. They had already eaten two large pizzas by themselves and were starting on four different flavors of ice cream. Besides the Round Rock sheriff and his deputies, four men from the FBI also joined the party. Then Sheriff Weaver arrived from Springdale, along with all the parents of the children.

"My family and I will be forever grateful," Tom Worthington said, covering his eye with a cold pack that Billy's father, Dr. Renner, had given him. Dr. Renner had also cleaned and bandaged the wounds on the young man's cheek and hand. "First the son saves me, and now the father binds up my wounds."

"I'm glad to do it," Dr. Renner said with a smile. He snapped his black bag shut and took a piece of pizza offered to him by Billy.

Over pizza and ice cream and lots of sodas, the parents and the police officers learned the real story about how the Home School Detectives foiled another crime. Each child had something to contribute, though Billy had the most to tell. As the story unfolded, the parents looked at each other and their children with total surprise bordering on shock. Tom Worthington was the most surprised of all to hear the story. He shook his head in amazement after Billy got through speaking.

"I still don't understand how this whole thing got started," Mrs. Renner said slowly.

"Jeremy Worthington, my cousin, was the mastermind," Tom said angrily. "Or at least he thought he was the mastermind. I think Mr. Wu and his friends would have double-crossed Jeremy and probably killed him."

"Jeremy is the guy with the red beard, right?" Billy asked.

"That's correct," Tom said. "Apparently he was jealous of me and worried that I would take over the company. I left home several years ago. I flunked out of college. I drifted around and wasted a lot of my father's money. I even got in trouble with the law. I stole a car one night when I got drunk. I got caught, went to jail, and my family was terribly embarrassed. But while I was in jail, some men visited me and told me about Jesus. I studied the Bible with them for several weeks. Eventually I realized how much I needed God. I became a Christian. God really changed me.

"But I don't think my family really believed me because I had disappointed them so many times before," Tom said softly. "When I came home, I told my father I just wanted to work in the factory like any other worker. I didn't want any special favors. He agreed. At that time, Jeremy was manager of the plant. He was jealous of me from the beginning and tried to make my life as hard as possible.

"But after a few years, my father could see that I really was different. He promoted me and helped me study and learn more about microprocessors and the cutting-edge technology that Worthington had developed. He put me in charge of the new Z-5000 project. I had good people working with me, and we did well. The product was a great success. We knew the new chip would earn millions of dollars. Then two things happened. My father got sick and Jeremy hatched a plan."

"Where is your father?" Billy asked. "That big house seemed awful empty."

"He's at the Mayo Clinic in Minnesota," Tom said. "My mother is up there with him. He's being treated for cancer. He may die soon. The doctors give him two months to live."

"I'm sorry to hear that," Billy said.

"So was my cousin, Jeremy," Tom said, nodding. "He was afraid my father would leave the company to me since I'm his son. Jeremy probably felt like he would be left out. So he began his scheme."

"To steal the computer chips?" Emily asked.

"He didn't directly steal anything," Tom replied. "He had Mr. Wu, who's part of an organized crime group in Hong Kong, approach me. Mr. Wu offered me two million dollars cash if I would help him steal chips and the chip technology. He promised me that it would look like the crime family did it, not me. As you may know, theft of computer chips is becoming quite common these days. He wanted me to steal six million dollars' worth of chips from my own company."

"Why did they think you would go along with a plan like that?" Billy asked.

"Jeremy was convinced I was still a thief at heart," Tom said. "He didn't know my heart has really been changed since I became a Christian. He was so blinded by his jealousy that he thought I would really try to steal the chips. But since he was working with Mr. Wu's group, Jeremy planned to have them double-cross me. They planned to kill me or make me take the fall for stealing the chips. Either way, I would be out of the picture, and Jeremy would inherit the company from my father. He also had a deal with Mr. Wu where he would get the two million dollars Mr. Wu had originally promised to me. Jeremy had it all worked out. After the robbery, he would have everything and I would have nothing."

"But you never planned to steal the chips," Billy said.

"No," Tom said. "As soon as Mr. Wu approached me, I contacted the FBI. They wanted to catch Mr. Wu and his friends. I agreed to help them. I secretly loaded up a truckful of the Z-5000 chips and stored them at an old warehouse in Springdale. No one thought I would move so fast. I contacted Mr. Wu and he planned to meet me and make an exchange. I would give him a few sample boxes of chips and a key and map to the warehouse. I had already told the FBI where I had stored the truck. They were staked out there waiting for Mr. Wu and his men to arrive. They planned to follow the truck all the way to the coast, where it was to be loaded on a ship going to Hong Kong. At that point they planned to arrest as many people as possible. It was a good plan."

"What happened then?" Billy asked.

"Jeremy got too eager," Tom said. "This morning when I was on my way to make the exchange, I saw Jeremy's car parked by the Dairy Queen. I also saw Chan inside his car. When I saw Chan, I knew Jeremy was in on the robbery some way, and I got scared. At the last minute, Mr. Wu changed the meeting place from the Springdale park to the alley where you children saw me. I was so upset, I dropped the car phone in my limousine. It broke. Because we were on a very tight schedule, I didn't have time to notify the FBI from a pay phone. I was praying hard because I was so scared.

"When I got to the alley, I put the box of chips with the map and key in the dumpster as a safeguard. I wanted to buy some time. Carl Boone, the man in the cowboy hat, got antsy. He only gave me part of the money and then insisted I go with him and Chan to meet with Mr. Wu. Then I noticed the front of Jeremy's car down at the end of the alley. I knew something bad was about to happen, so I tried to run.

"Carl and Chan ran me off the road in Springdale, and the limousine crashed. Chan knocked me out with his pistol. I don't remember what happened until I woke up in the pickup truck way out in the country. Chan knocked me around quite a bit until I finally told him where I put the other two boxes of chips and the key and map."

"This is what they were after the whole time," Billy said, proudly holding up the plastic bag with the map and warehouse key. "I found it at the dump and kept it in my pocket."

"That's right," Tom said. "None of us knew the dumpsters were being picked up this morning. Jeremy went to the alley to look for the chips. When he realized he'd been found out in a lie by Emily and the others, he panicked and kidnapped them. I didn't know that the kids were involved at all until they locked us up together in the old laundry room. Then, it was up to Billy to rescue us all."

Billy beamed at the attention. Josh handed him a second bowl of ice cream, which Billy gladly took.

"This young man certainly kept his head clear under pressure," said FBI agent Dan Larson to Billy. "All of you should be proud. We've been after Mr. Wu and his group for several years. They're a vicious, powerful crime group. He'll be in jail for a long, long time after we get through with this case. And so will Jeremy Worthington."

"God was watching out after you children," Mrs. Renner said, shaking her head. "I can't believe that when you left the house this morning, all I thought you were going to do was a little research down at the *Springdale Gazette*."

"God was watching out for all of us," Tom Worthington said with a painful smile. "I've been praying since early this morning that God would make this thing turn out okay. I must admit, though, I wondered after a while if he was really going to answer that prayer. I was scared that I wouldn't ever see tomorrow."

"I was really scared too," Billy said seriously. "But there is a good side to this whole thing."

"You mean that we didn't get kidnapped and shipped to Hong Kong?" Josh asked.

"Well, that was good, but that's not what I mean," Billy replied.

"You mean because you helped prevent a robbery?" Carlos asked.

"That was okay too, but that's not what I mean," Billy admitted.

"Well, you probably helped save my life," Tom Worthington said gratefully.

"And our lives too," Rebecca added.

"Yeah, I'm glad about that too," Billy said. "But there's something even better."

"What is it, then?" Dr. Renner asked his son. "What could be better than all those things?"

"I'm glad things turned out the way they did and that we're all safe," Billy said. Then he smiled. "But the best thing is that I learned to climb trees today and I'm not afraid of heights anymore. And you know what that means, don't you, Dad?"

Dr. Renner laughed, nodding his head.

"Now you can build that tree house you've been promising," Billy said. "You said that once I could be up high without being afraid, you would build us a tree house."

"We'll start tomorrow, son," Dr. Renner said with a smile.

"And I'll be right up there helping you," Billy said. He looked at his friends and grinned broadly. "Just you wait and see. I'll climb higher than anyone in the whole neighborhood."

"I believe it," Dr. Renner said, shaking his head. "I believe every word you say."

Don't miss the next book
in the Home School Detectives
series!

Here's a preview of
John Bibee's
*The Mystery of
the Mexican Graveyard.*

Chapter One

The Ghost in the Graveyard

C arlos and Julie Brown and their friends were walking up a narrow cobblestone street in the little Mexican town of Santiago when they heard the scream. They were near the top of the hill by an old abandoned church. The church stood on the land next door to the orphanage. They paused, listening. All they heard was the wind, which had picked up rapidly since they had left the birthday party fifteen minutes earlier.

The party for one of the children at the orphanage had been in the town plaza. The customs at a Mexican birthday were different from the birthday parties back in Springdale, but Carlos and his sister had just as much fun. Carlos himself had delivered the final blow to the large colorful piñata which spilled candy out all over the ground. The only drawback was that he had been blindfolded. As soon as the piñata burst, all the other children had rushed in and scooped up most of the candy before Carlos could rip off the mask and join them. He had only gotten three pieces of candy, while the other children's hands and pockets were bulging with the sweet treasures.

Still, he was proud that he had delivered the final blow to the papier-mâché piñata, which was shaped like a giant parrot. All the other children had cheered as he had swung the broom handle. Unfortunately, as soon as the candy was picked up, lightning flashed and thunder rumbled in the distance. During the party, dark clouds had moved across the mountains and over the little seaside town. The party had broken up. Carlos and Julie and several other kids had decided to walk back to the orphanage.

"We can beat the rain," Carlos had told his father and mother. "Besides, even if it does rain, we'll just get a little bit wet. Please, please, please?"

A few moments later, Carlos and the others were climbing up the winding street to the top of the hill. The children had stopped to catch their breath when they heard the scream.

"It came from the church."

"No, from behind the church," Julie said. "From the cemetery."

Now everyone forgot the storm and the party. Each child stared into the darkness. A light flashed behind the old church building among the graves. All the children looked toward the light. Carlos was sure he saw a shadowy shape moving among the old gravestones. The dark clouds overhead made the night that much darker and lonelier. A sudden gust of wind blew dust across the street. Lightning flashed in the distance, followed by a slow rumbling of thunder. But as soon as the thunder stopped, they heard the low wailing again.

"What was that?" Carlos asked the others.

"I don't know," Miguel replied. "It sounded awful, like someone could be dying. Maybe it's someone from the graves."

"¡Los muertos, los muertos!" Maria cried fearfully. "Lo están haciendo otra vez." The nine-year-old girl began to tug at Miguel's hand, pulling her older brother away from the old church. Her dark eyes were fixed on the shadowy graves in the distant cemetery.

" 'Los muertos'?" Carlos asked, trying to remember what the words meant.

" 'The dead people,' " Julie replied. "She said, 'They're doing it again.' "

"The dead people are doing what again?" Carlos asked in surprise. "How can dead people do anything, let alone do it again?"

Even though Carlos had been born in Mexico, Julie was the one who knew more Spanish. When he was very young, his parents had died. Carlos had been adopted by Pastor Brown and his family. He never even knew anything about Mexico until he was five years old, when the Browns returned to Santiago to help out the people at the orphanage.

Every year since then, the Springdale Community Church sent a team of people to Santiago to work in the orphanage and in the town of Santiago, which was on the eastern coast of Mexico, north of Veracruz. Carlos and Julie loved being part of the missions trips. There was always lots of hard work, but they enjoyed being in another country.

During that week the young people and adults from Springdale had helped paint the entire orphanage, inside and out. On some days, the young people from the Springdale church had sung in the town plaza and acted out skits in Spanish and English. Earlier that morning, all the other families had begun the trip back home to Springdale, leaving only Carlos and his family. His dad had decided to stay a few more days to help Pastor Pablo. Hearing the strange crying voices made Carlos wish he was safe with the others on their way to the United States. Another shriek split the air. Carlos jerked back. Julie shivered.

"Los muertos gritan," Maria moaned.

"Dead people don't make sounds." Carlos peered into the shadows behind the old mission. Carlos, who wanted to be a scientist when he got older, always tried to understand things in a logical, scientific manner.

"What about ghosts?" Maria asked.

"Do ghosts make sounds?" Julie asked with concern.

"I believe in the Holy Ghost, which is another name for the Holy Spirit," Carlos said. "But I don't believe in ghosts that float around and scare people. That voice sounded human."

"It sounded weird to me," Julie said.

"But ghosts are the spirits of dead people, aren't they?" Miguel replied. "It could be a ghost. The kids in the orphanage are talking about ghosts. Some have seen strange things. Others have heard noises."

"Maybe they were dreaming. I haven't heard anyone talk about this before," Carlos said skeptically.

"No one talks about it much," Miguel said uneasily. "This last week everyone was busy with painting and doing things with their church friends from Springdale. I don't think anyone saw or heard the ghost the whole time."

"I haven't heard Pastor Pablo talk about any ghosts,"

"Pastor Pablo doesn't want the little ones to get scared since we all live next door to the old church," Miguel replied.

"But we are scared," Maria said. She spoke English slowly, trying not to make mistakes. The little girl's large brown eyes returned to the shadowy darkness behind the old church.

The church and the orphanage were at the north end of the town on a small foothill of the mountains overlooking the bay. Most nights you could see the moonlight dancing on the water. But this night was too dark. Carlos could smell the salty sea air as another gust of wind cut through the dark night.

"Woooooo!" a voice yelled. Everyone but Carlos screamed as they turned around. Miguel was already running down the street.

"Flaco!" Julie yelled. "You scared us!"

"I know," laughed a tall skinny boy. He smiled at everyone. Then he reached down to scratch his ankle. His bare feet were dirty. The orphanage provided all the children with shoes, but Flaco never wore them. "Look at poor Miguel run. He looks like a jackrabbit being chased by a coyote."

"That's not funny, Flaco," Maria said, her dark eyes flashing. "You shouldn't sneak up on us like that. You know that scares us."

"I was just running after Roberto," Flaco said, still grinning, enjoying the fear he had caused in the others. "He said he was going to catch up with you guys."

"That's a lie," Miguel said. "Roberto isn't with us."

"He told me he was going with you guys," Flaco insisted.

"You're just trying to scare us," Maria accused. "You always lie or make excuses."

"I do not!" Flaco shot back angrily. "Can I help it if you babies get scared in the dark?"

babies get scared in the dark?"

Carlos didn't say anything. He didn't really like Flaco. In fact, not many of the children in the orphanage liked the tall skinny boy because he often said cruel things or played mean jokes on the others. He had only been at the orphanage six months and hadn't made many friends. Several children had complained about Flaco to Pastor Pablo. Even though he had been in trouble several times with the pastor, once even for stealing, Flaco didn't seem to change his angry ways. Earlier that week, Emily Morgan's portable radio and cassette player had disappeared. No one could prove he had stolen it, but everyone, including Carlos, suspected Flaco. Emily had left that morning without recovering the cassette player.

"Chi chi chi chi," Flaco said, flapping his arms like a bird. He laughed and pointed to Miguel.

"We aren't scared," Miguel shot back as he returned to the group.

"You ran like the little bird you are," Flaco replied with a smug smile. "We all saw you."

"You be quiet," Miguel said fiercely.

"Are you going to fight me?" Flaco asked angrily. He made his hands into fists as he stepped toward Miguel. He towered over the younger boy. Miguel looked mad enough to fight, but he knew he wouldn't have a chance. He took a step back and looked at the ground in shame.

"See, you are a little chicken, a *pollito*," Flaco said with disgust. Then he turned to Carlos. "Do you want to fight with me?"

"I'm not looking for a fight," Carlos said. He felt his anger building.

"Are you a little *pollito* too?" Flaco asked, smiling his

smug smile.

"Carlos isn't afraid of you," Julie said hotly.

"So your big sister will fight for you?" Flaco said. "Is that how they do it in the United States? The sisters fight for their *pollito* brothers?"

"Quit calling me a *pollito*," Carlos replied. He took a step toward the older boy.

"What are you going to do about it?" Flaco demanded. "Maybe I should ask your sister. She's the fighter in the family."

"I'm not afraid of big mouths like you," Carlos said, standing up straighter. Flaco smiled.

The tall skinny boy was about to make a reply when it happened. A gust of wind shook the leaves in the trees, and an eerie green light flashed in the darkness among the gravestones. All the children saw the light briefly before it was smothered by the darkness.

"You saw that, didn't you?" Miguel asked, his lips quivering.

"¡Los muertos!" Maria shuddered.

"I think we should get out of here," Julie said nervously.

"Maybe," Carlos said, still staring into the darkness.

Flaco looked surprised and then scared. The older boy stared fearfully at the darkness. He looked back at the others. His whole attitude had changed.

"It *is* true," Flaco said softly. "I thought the other kids were scared or making up stories."

"They were scared for a reason," Miguel replied.

"We better get back to the orphanage," Carlos said.

"But the ghost is near the fence!" Flaco said. "We'd have to walk right by it!"

"That's the only way," Carlos insisted. He took a few steps up the road toward the church and graveyard. His feet were the only ones making sounds. He turned and looked around. Julie and the others stood together in a tight little group, as if their feet were planted in the road. Even Flaco was standing as close as he could get to the other children.

"Come on," Carlos said. "Let's get home before—"

"Ooooooooooiiiiiiiiieeeeeee!" a voice cried out in the darkness. Carlos whirled around. The glowing, eerie green figure was closer. This time they could see it more clearly. The vaguely human shape stood right at the old broken iron gate of the cemetery. Carlos looked and blinked his eyes. Where there should have been feet was just darkness. The ghost appeared to be floating two feet above the ground. When it passed through the half-open gate and came closer, Carlos had seen enough.

Screams filled the air. Carlos turned around to run. The others were already speeding down the road as fast as they could go, shrieking at the top of their lungs. Carlos didn't look back. He ran as fast as he could go and caught up with the group. None of them stopped running until they reached the plaza in town.

Also by John Bibee
THE SPIRIT FLYER SERIES

During the course of a year, the ordinary town of Centerville
becomes the setting for some extraordinary events.
When several children discover that Spirit Flyer bicycles
possess strange and wondrous powers, they are thrust
into a conflict with Goliath Industries—with the
fate of the town in the balance.

Available from your local bookstore or

InterVarsity Press
Downers Grove, Illinois 60515